To C
with
from
D1827560

THREE WOMEN

THREE WOMEN

Daphne Glazer

PIATKUS

First published in Great Britain in 1984 by
Judy Piatkus (Publishers) Limited of London

Typeset by Phoenix Photosetting, Chatham

Printed and bound in Great Britain by
Mackays of Chatham Ltd

ISBN 0 86188 440 X

Chapter 1

It wasn't as though it had just started happening. In fact it had been going on for years. He was determined to finish her and she knew it.

The light in the hall was brownish and dim. They were separated from each other by three-piece suites, 'wernicke' bookcases, Minton tea sets and dinner services set out on a big mahogany table, all manner of upholstered armchairs, carpets, sideboards and wardrobes.

Linda could only see the top of his head. His slicked-up, oiled hair gleamed, and a camel-coated shoulder wedged itself against a wardrobe.

Moffat, the auctioneer, was surveying them with his clever half-smile. He liked to jolly them along, urge them into a rash commitment by his quick repartee and deft sliding from one pound to the next before anybody had realised it.

'Now this is quite a fine Persian carpet – do I have any offers? Who'd like to start me off – come on, start me off! This looks like something for you, Mr Brocklesby.'

Linda heard Moffat's deference, and sniffed, taking a deep drag on her spindly roll-up. 'Bastard,' she

1

muttered under her breath. Moffat wouldn't look in her direction, she didn't expect him to. He disapproved of her: most did. She knew what he was thinking: 'Ugly old cow!' It pleased her.

'Right, let's start – you can see for yourselves –' Moffat was twinkling, 'hold it up, boys. The ladies and gentlemen want to see what they're buying now, don't they?'

Linda knew. She had taken it in at a glance, the smudgy pinks and blues, the mysterious navy. No, things rarely escaped Linda's cod-cold stare. Now she was watching Moffat's mouth and the play of his hands.

They were coming to the end of the auction. It had been a whole day of sitting about on the suites waiting to be auctioned, peering at cases of dusty books, inspecting plates for cracks and chips, always keeping an ear open for the magic numbers. The cold was intense and struck up through the floor, numbing your feet. Moffat's flat voice had droned on throughout and Linda had kept popping back. She was a regular and knew the pattern. Now, waiting, her hunting instinct had been roused. She was ready.

Off it went. It was almost like the start of a horse-race. Moffat's voice moved into a eldritch sing-song. 'Twenty . . . do I hear twenty-five . . . thirty, thirty-five, forty –' His little dark eyes birded about the motionless mass beneath his rostrum.

They were over the hundred mark now. He knew the faces to concentrate on. Linda had listened to the early cataract spasmodically. Her interest began to perk up as the casuals retired, leaving the hard core. She began making herself another roll-up, nipping the tobacco deftly out of her tin which she had placed on the top of a sideboard. Drip, drip, she ran the Old Holborn squiggles onto the liquorice paper. This was her element.

'One hundred and fifty – do I hear one five five?' Brocklesby's head was half-turned. He was pretending elaborately not to be doing anything but his little finger twitched and Moffat watched it.

Up it went again. Five, five woven together by the incantation. Moffat was a high-priest muttering a chant. They were leading to a climax. There would be a spurt of flame, a gigantic explosion. The huddled faces spitted thin smoke, chewed gum, dusted down jackets and coats, fidgeted and then waited. Moving up.

'Two – did I hear two five? Did I? Come on, Mr Brocklesby – what's happening to you?'

'Two fifteen.'

Heads shot round to examine the speaker. What a strange, flat, insistent voice! Linda pressed on. She was aware only of the ripple of excitement. They had noticed that she had laid down a challenge by doubling the bid.

This was a game at which Linda excelled. You could do all manner of things. Once you had ascertained that a rival wanted a certain object, lusted after it even, and was prepared to sacrifice more than its worth, you shot up the bidding, but you must extricate yourself carefully. It would be disastrous to be caught out, though it could happen. You must know the exact moment to cease bidding.

Brocklesby wanted the carpet. Linda wanted the carpet. Both knew it.

It was going in tens now much to Moffat's satisfaction. The hall was silent except for the harsh scrape of a cough and the distant thunder of lorries on the road outside. Linda had promised Sue she'd try to get the carpet and that made it even more important.

Brocklesby's finger twitched. He was not so off-hand now, he daren't be. Linda nodded. A wire of tension

3

linked them, it was Moffat's birdy gaze. Back and forth.

'Now Mr Brocklesby, do I take it you've finished – do I? Come on, another ten – it's a fine carpet, there's no doubt. A fine carpet. Can I say ten? Would you like to have another look at it?' a gentle cajoling, a heavy gambol in the hay. 'Mr Brocklesby, your last word?'

Heads turned to the back of the room and the camel coat.

Oh, Linda knew it, camel in winter, white Burberry in summer, the heavy gold signet ring flashing on the little finger. He made her think of whisky and port, drunk in men's clubs with maroon velvet curtains and smokers' armchairs.

'That's it then – to Mrs Peach at £450 . . .'

Chattering suddenly broke loose. People began to shift about, coughing and cold and creased, released by a drama which they sensed but couldn't understand. They had witnessed something, but what, they weren't sure.

With the help of Tommy, one of Moffat's lads, Linda heaved up the precious sausage of carpet onto her shoulder and then strode out of the auction gallery to her bicycle and cart which were parked outside.

'It'll just about go on there, I reckon,' Linda said, her voice low with satisfaction. Four fifty, not bad – and there was the triumph of having defeated Brocklesby. She had not seen his face. His big white Jag would be parked at the back of the building. 'Nasty brute,' she thought.

Tommy helped her stow the carpet away. She smiled grimly at him. He nodded at her warily.

Linda pedalled into the main stream of traffic. She was in an extraordinarily good mood and hummed as she witched along past Monument Fisheries and the

4

doric columns of the art gallery next door, and took a splendid swing by Queen Vickie perched on the public lavs. The cold February wind caused her pewter hair to stream in wild weedy strands about her head. In places it had the brassy glare of an old smoker's moustache.

One Persian carpet, one pink, baby-blue, gentian-blue fabric of dreams. You could lose half a day following the delights of its twirls and jewelled centres. Cross-legged men in hareem pants had sat bare-footed twining spindles. She could smell incense and hear husky chanting. Gold filigree work glittered against enamelled surfaces, and the blue was the rich vestial sapphire of a madonna's robe or a Mediterranean summer sea.

Brocklesby would hit back, of that there wasn't the slightest doubt. Let him do his worst! Nothing could be much more unpleasant than 'The Fall'. She always called that event 'The Fall' privately. It had happened when she had first been starting out on her tat-adventure and had been running her 'Rainbow Palace'. The Palace had been an old shop in a slice of brick house which had once belonged to a continuous brick terrace. The town had many such but they were slowly being demolished by Brocklesby Enterprises – Dale Brocklesby's brother, Sam. He and another contractor had a virtual monopoly of the town's demolition work. This meant that they could get their hands on exquisite old Robinson fireplaces. People had suddenly realized what she had known for a long time, that those twining Art Nouveau tulips and lemon flowers glowing on a scarlet field of tiles were highly decorative and very precious. Oh, she had a fair idea of what Brocklesby had misappropriated: things had a habit of finding their way into Dale Brocklesby's antique shop. Many were shipped to America or Holland.

5

Sam Brocklesby's lads had moved in bulldozers and caterpillars and a curiously menacing American ex-army truck which was brown with a white star on its side. Soon the whole area had been reduced to a heap of rubble – just piles and piles of bricks with mortar still sticking to them. Big ugly skips had been dumped in the middle of that flotsam. Dust and smoke had mushroomed like an atomic cloud. Lads, rough-necks in old combat gear, ranged about the area with a daemonic intensity. They were attacking the buildings and drawing out their entrails in the same way that small children set about the flattening of painstakingly-built sandcastles.

Linda had seen the savage glee on their faces. 'Vultures'. Those piles of rubble were the dreams of families long since dead and gone. She had paused, gazing out over the sea of debris. 'And now,' she thought, 'the council will build a lot of hateful concrete boxes with plots of clay at the front and not a tree or a blade of grass in sight, metal clothes poles in identical lines – all slapped up against one another and walls so thin you can hear every row and every kiss in the next bedroom – and every fart for that matter.'

In the middle of all this had stood the Rainbow Palace. On fine days she'd let her wares spill out onto the pavement: glass cake-stands, earthernware bread pansions, old enamel saucepans, cotton nightdresses and grandad shirts, 1940s beaver and squirrel coats, feather boas, flowered plates and jugs, old prams, costume jewellery, clip-on earrings, dressing-tables, and chests of drawers – heaps and heaps of rummaging junk. And the passers-by would come and browse amongst it, turning things over thoughtfully. It had attracted people from all the terraces nearby and from much wider a field.

6

Then suddenly Brocklesby's mob had plunged down upon it. She'd appealed to the Council. No. The Rainbow Palace was to be demolished. How did she think that her shop could hold up the force of change? She had dug her heels in. It hadn't made any difference.

'Madam, if you don't shift your junk, it'll all go in the skip with the bricks and mortar when we fetch it down.'

Big fleshy-faced men with greased-back hair and pale eyes had barged in. She'd imagined Dale's satisfaction – he'd thought she was an ugly excrescence, something to be rubbed off, removed from view, to be replaced by a concrete box with carefully sanitized inmates.

But oh no, it hadn't finished her, not on your life! Realizing that there could be no possible stay of execution, she had cast about for about other premises and had found her present place, 'The Emporium' in a terrace not far away. With Tom and Cordelia helping, she had shifted everything in a hired van. On the morning of the demolition she had been there to watch the giant claws and the great cast-iron ball clonking round on its chain as it clobbered the tall slice of house. In a shower of bricks and thick dust the Rainbow Palace had tumbled down. Pieces of twisted metal like contorted limbs had lain amongst heaps of rubble and broken window frames.

By the end of the day it had disappeared as though it had never been there. Late in the afternoon Linda had bicycled over to Brocklesby's shop and had stood with her nose pressed to the glass part of the door and had pulled the most horrific face she could manage. She imagined herself to be one of those repellent tropical fish with a big head, rubbery spines, a jagged tail and malevolent gold eyes. He couldn't quite believe it and so she had stuck her tongue out and waggled her ears.

7

On she bicycled, by rows of little shops, bakeries, newsagents, fish-shops, greengrocers', betting shops, allowing herself to grin at the memory of it. His jaw had dropped. She had read disbelief in his eyes. He did things differently from her. He liked to have one or two choice things – maybe a Victorian grandfather chair with spindly cabriole legs and a matching lady's chair, both upholstered in shell-coloured velvet displayed in his window and inside the shop you'd find all manner of objets d'art – not a single one bearing a price tag. There were pieces of Royal Doulton standing alone on shelves, glassy mahogany dining tables laid with silver and Meissen dinner services: that was his shop-front, the genteel side, meant to dazzle. He liked to preside there, rubbing his pale, plump hands and jerking in and out of the back premises like a cuckoo when the clock's about to chime. Of course that was if he sensed he might be getting a customer. And then there was his tie-tweaking routine, or the primping up his navy-blue and maroon spotted cravat. Navy-blue-suited, he would preen amongst his choicest pieces.

'What a willy,' Linda thought, panting as she met the gusts of wind from the estuary. What would Sue think of the carpet? She'd be ecstatic because she hadn't really expected to get it. That was one of the marvellous things about auctions, you never knew what to expect. Linda liked the unpredictable, the challenging.

Sue's light was on – good, she must be back. Linda left her bike in the road and trudged up to the front door.

Chapter 2

Sue Edwards was trying to wind down. She drifted to and fro amongst the twining monsteras, grape ivies, rubber plants and scented geraniums, plugging in her electric kettle and ruminating on what had happened that day. First there had been the annoyance of trying to explain short-story writing whilst an electric drill droned and shrieked in the room immediately below where she had been teaching.

'So you see, the younger couple merely reflect the development of the older one –' rasp, rumble, bang! 'Damnation, do I have to . . . is this what teaching's about? Do you think I'm being too sensitive?' She liked to have their approval, because she loved them – yes, she really did. There was daft Billy, a thin moony lad, with a pale face who wanted to talk about psychiatrists, and Eve, dark and pretty in her thirties. She was clever in an unusual way and like lots of married women had never had a proper chance. Her essays gave Sue pleasure, a thrill of acknowledgement: that's right, exactly right – beautiful! Bunty, big-breasted, bespectacled, orange-haired, in her late twenties, a girl who was bringing up a baby single-handed and had a boundless enthusiasm for life: she painted, was rough, rumbustious and also quite extraordinary. She could see them all – and the nervous woman, Betty, who had shoulder-length, dyed black hair and wore tropical make-up and had ruby-red lips and whose asthma squeaked and didn't match her beauty-chorus get-up. Then she had stormed downstairs onto the landing below and into the room beneath.

'I can't teach with this racket going on all the time!'

The electrician, a young chap with brooding shoulders, had stopped for a moment on his platform, his hand holding the drill suspended. Oddly phallic things drills, she had reflected whilst continuing to fume.

'Can't help it – my job!'

'You wouldn't stand for this in industry, would you? It would be all out, wouldn't it? Listen – no heating, no lighting in the staff-room for two weeks and every bloody lesson this hassle –'

She had heard the scream of her own voice and saw his lazy smile. He thought she was a nutter – she could tell that. He was also experiencing some sort of pleasure, because he had the upper-hand, and as he secretly considered himself to be her social inferior the victory was doubly sweet. She could have dragged him down and impaled him on his own great whining drill.

Steadily she poured water into the teapot. Lemon-scented tea. Hmm, she sniffed it. She would savour each mouthful, drinking it from a china cup, one of her Rainbow Palace purchases.

Reclining on her blue velvet chaise-longue, she sipped her tea and surveyed the room. It was gradually beginning to emerge as she would want it to be. She had spent all that last summer stripping wallpaper off, using filler to stuff the cracks in the crumbling plaster. She had bought new skirting-board, old fireplaces, tiled ones . . . it would be a room like the sea – turquoise-blue white – entrapping, caressing, comforting: at once remote and intimate.

She leaned back against velvet cushions. Her shoulder-length spiny hair was a forest of winter branches. Her body was long and narrowish under the white silk shirt with the pearl buttons.

What was all this about? She was in a strange dreamy state and had been for a long time. Her dreams filled the day-time too. She knew herself to be an obsessional type and must deal with whatever was preoccupying her exclusively and exhaustively.

Now she was being prickled by the irritation of having had to teach in impossible situations with drills droning and apprentice plumbers and brickies effing and blinding and scraping their feet on wood-block floors when she was giving an English language class next door.

'I want some beautiful piece of furniture,' she thought, surveying the full length of her room, the softly swaying beaded shades, the silver Eros bearing his white globe so eloquently. She let her gaze rest on the thrust of his arm. She would have liked an alabaster discus thrower on a marble plinth. Perhaps Linda would unearth something somewhere.

This house had been a venture which she had arrived at only after a long period of shifting about. There had been a time when she could not have envisaged buying property. She had been content to remain a flat-dweller indefinitely. But a sudden change had taken place in her. It had, she felt, been something to do with Gary Martin. Until his appearance her life had been governed by other factors. Gary still seemed to be around in some irritating and indefinable way. Sue lay back, took a glug of tea and watched the bare twigs moving behind the long window.

She had met him in the Victorian conservatory – a place

11

of dreams. It drew her regularly and was in fact only a five-minute walk away. On winter day she had gone there, looking for a touch of the exotic. She was wandering amongst the massed banks of blue and purple hyacinths whose scent had made her almost dizzy. Banana trees, giant rubber-plants, monsteras, a date palm, kentias – all had been pressing up towards the arch of glass, and from the middle had come the twittering and trilling of the aviary.

It was in the second house by the goldfish pond that she had turned to find the young man behind her – white faced, with permed blond hair, a hunching ungainly body fastened into a flier's jacket. Life had ploughed his face already and he looked haggard.

'Gor a light?'

'Maybe'.

He had annoyed her simply by being there and accosting her in that jade wilderness. The two mynah birds screeched and honked, stirring up wild echoes. In the aquaria set into the wall the tiny fishes glittered silver and mother of pearl. Water trickled over a stone shelf and plopped onto pebbles. It was warm in there and secret. She had rummaged in her bag. 'Here.' He had taken the matches slowly from her hand, looking into her face at the same time and smiling crookedly. She had glimpsed a certain wrecked beauty and it had made the excitement leap in her like some electric charge. She had looked quickly away. He had set about making himself a roll-up. 'Hold us that –' he had proffered his tobacco tin. 'Want one?' She'd nodded.

They had sat for a while on the wooden seat gazing at the small birds darting amid the twining olive green jungle. Light gleamed on glass and water and spilled over pebbles like oil.

Later he had walked beside her back to her flat in a tree-lined avenue.

12

A sailor. He had sat watching her making tea in that other room which she had rarely dusted and which was packed with 1920s lamps, prints, bracket-footed chests. There had been a gold-eyed barn owl beaconing from its glass case. She remembered everything about it – the awfulness of her excitement. Here it was so simple – a young man whom she did not know, tall, hunched, his body a thin shaft in jeans, flier's jacket and lean shirt, his blue eyes hot and swimmy. She had always liked the idea of impersonal encounters. You might read of them in novels or see them in films: woman encounters man in train, no word is spoken, they make love and part instantly. The ideal would have been a window-cleaner. She could see it quite clearly. Unfortunately, though, all the window-cleaners she knew were either too decrepit or had some obvious draw-back like loose false teeth or gormlessness which must preclude such an encounter. Anyway, the sailor had sat there, staring at her and the room had been filled with the hulking presence of passion. She did not believe in passion but there was nevertheless this thrilling of the senses to which some might have given that name.

He had told her about the sea, whilst she sprawled opposite him, smoked and said 'ja' periodically. Foreign parts, tropical islands, brothels, dope – he and his companions had been high all the time on something. She had imagined a ship packed with lurching blue figures and had pressed him for more brothel details – brothels seemed so stagey, so aesthetically deodorised and unpleasant, rather an insult in fact. He had laughed. She had noticed how pointed and cruel his teeth seemed.

And of course he had come across to her. The light had been behind him and she had seen his features only

13

as an indistinct blur, but that had rendered them in a way more poignant and lost – a Botticelli angel, or one of Milton's fallen angels. He had lost his purity but in another sense could not lose it.

Suddenly there was a sharp ring on the door-bell. She jumped, almost dropping the china cup.

'Sue, Sue!'

Linda's strange ragged outline appeared behind the frosted arabesques in the top half of the door.

'Look! I've got it!'

Sue ran out of the front porch to the road where Linda's cart waited.

'I nearly didn't – was a very close-run thing.'

'Fantastic!' She leapt in the air and did a wild dance. Then they were bringing in the carpet, one to either end. Breathlessly Sue unrolled it in her embryonic sitting-room. It lay there, showing off its dusky pinks and smudged blues.

'Christ, it's beautiful – it's brilliant – I love it, I love it! What do you think? Do you like it?'

'Of course I do or I wouldn't have got it for you, would I – four hundred and fifty.'

'That's good, isn't it?'

'Yeah, I told you –' Linda's well-shaped hands were searching inside her hidden pockets for her tobacco tin and the end of a roll-up she had never managed to finish.

'Tea?'

'Wouldn't go astray.'

They sat on the chaise-longue side by side, drinking fragrant tea and staring at the carpet. Linda recounted the day's drama.

'Great conceited twerp. Oh aye, he thought he'd get it – but did he! Mind you, we'll hear more of that, you watch!' Linda's flat, unlined face sank deeper into

14

inscrutability, her eyes behind their pink-framed lenses narrowed and seemed to disappear almost under the puffy folds of flesh. They laughed comfortably together. Most days they shared tales of on-going feuds.

'What a day!' Sue groaned. 'I'm glad this has arrived – it's really cheered me up. You find you spend your life struggling to make yourself heard and trying to manage with one text-book per three people and then there's one tiny little radiator in a room like a barn – they say it used to be the old orphanage and they found the skeletons of children under the floor-boards. It feels like it! I suppose any funds there are, go on prestige projects like new carpets for some prick's office. . . .' Disgustedly she began making herself another roll-up.

'Sign of the times,' Linda grunted, dabbing her ash into an Art Deco ashtray. 'I don't know what young Cordelia's going to do.'

Cordelia was sixteen and might have been thirty. She was big and beautiful, the colour of coffee-cream.

Just then they saw her face peering in at the sitting-room window.

'Come in!' Sue gesticulated.

They heard the crash of the front door and in swept Cordelia. She had her mother's big smooth face but it was lit by vivacity and the features were smaller. School uniform looked out of place on her. Out of school she mostly wore 1920s gear, little crêpe suits with square shoulders and angular hats darted with savage quills which you could imagine coming direct from the plumage of some fierce, glossy bird. She had a feather boa too. This person was like some voluptuous show-biz queen. Sue always expected her to open her mouth and start singing in a rich, grinding contralto or

15

doing a sinuous tap-dance. Her body was a big slinky tube. When she was dolled up in her 1920s dressed her belly and thighs were suggested distinctly and there was some atavistic resemblance to a butter-fat market mammy or an American blues singer.

'Hi!' Her yellow palms sprayed a salute.

'Like my new carpet?'

'Mm, nice colours . . . fab . . .' Cordelia went to lean on the mantlepiece. She was at the age where posing was very important. She stared at the carpet for a few minutes and then at her mother and Sue. 'I feel like making something gorgeous and yummy –'

'Well, why not?' Linda's slit eyes came up for a few seconds.

'It's just that there's this kid who'll probably drop in –'

'And?'

'And that might be okay –'

Linda was staring past her daughter at the fireplace. What was she going to do?

Sue couldn't stop admiring Cordelia. She was beautiful, exotic – somehow completely natural.

'Better go, I suppose,' Linda said and withdrew finally, Cordelia loping behind her. Sue was left to her own thoughts. Her evenings, when she wasn't teaching, were pleasant, unhurried times. She did what she liked, marked, read, knitted, occasionally watched TV, all in her kitchen, ensconced on her cart-whorled sofa and with her antique gas-fire roaring away.

The track of her thoughts would not be diverted: she had to work it through. It took its course like an illness. What was the illness this time? Gary Martin. She supposed that of the males who had briefly made their appearance in her life, he had involved her the most. She had never intended that he should. She missed the sex and didn't like to think of it. How odd it had been.

For months she had not bothered about him. She had given lectures, talked with colleagues, sat up all night with Linda over pots of tea or sometimes beer, visited her other friends – all pleasantly enough, and then there'd be a ring on the door-bell one day and he'd be back. And it had been like a fever. He wouldn't say anything but they'd go straight into the bedroom, or down on the rug before the fire. At those times she had suffered from an obsession for him. She had wanted to be touching him every moment, running her fingertips through his hair, putting her tongue in his ears. pressing her lips to his eyelids, the bridge of his nose, touching his shoulders, his hard body. The progress to his thighs had been slow, warm, fevered – such a frenzy amid animal fur and satin and velvet. Oh, she had loved his smell, which had been both resinous and bitter – of the earth and subject to decay. She had wanted to sap him, possess him, grind him to bits, bite him, suck him. Juices had filled her mouth and the area between her legs. Her pores had oozed moisture: all of her had been gushed out on him in an attempt to encompass whatever he was. But basically she had not wanted to know him.

She didn't like to conjure up those sensations any longer, because that way they turned into an unassuagable hunger. As she didn't believe in love or romance, what the hell did you name such a lunatic emotion?

He had married at sixteen – a shot-gun affair which had produced two children in quick succession. By twenty he had been through with marriage and ready for something else. From them on he had worn himself out in the relentless pursuit of a devastating sensation: once he thought he had it, it was gone.

There had been the most bitter rows between them:

17

'Put the kettle on, love – get us a cuppa!' 'What about you – do you think I'm the servant or something?' 'Snooty bitch!'

She had made him wash-up, clean her flat, prepare meals (a new sensation!) When he had come banging on the door, late on, drunk, she had bellowed through an open window, 'Oh piss off – come round when you can stand up!'

The Valkyrie hadn't been in it – looking back she must smile at the force of her rage. But the fact remained, in some obscure way she had wanted every bit of him, and from the intensity of their love-making she had supposed that there must be a certain exclusiveness between them. There had been weekends on the east coast, mad drives there on his motorbike when he had returned from sea, evenings in seaside hotels, drinking pints, knowing that they would later devour each other in the bedroom. But, but how big was that 'but'! In this constant struggle between the ebb and flow, she discovered he was screwing other women. When he was drunk he didn't mind. It could be anyone. That had hurt. She had tried to rationalise why she should be upset by it – she had said no strings, no strings whatsoever – but then, one often says the opposite of what one feels.

On it had gone, hiccuping and raging until the final scene when the bastard had gone beyond the point where she could forgive or wanted to. Basically she had thought to educate him, because he had been a rough diamond. He couldn't spell – okay, had difficulty in identifying a main verb – but he could think logically. So she had encouraged him. There had also been in him, and she had found that very attractive, the crusading zeal of old trade-unionists. At sea he had made himself a thorough nuisance because of it and

18

been threatened with dismissal. The word 'mutinous' had been mentioned.

Through her guidance he had ended up at an adult college. During the vacations he would turn up at her flat, until the one he didn't. No word, no sign. He had gone to Germany with a girl . . . and Sue had wanted something special. That thing she had been set on, had frightened him – or so it seemed.

Chapter 3

General Studies, first-year hairdressing apprentices.
She enjoyed teaching them. She wanted to help them,
make them more aware. What of? Of other possibilities, yes, that was it! When she thought of their certain
future she invariably felt appalled. It would be a quick
trot from the brief years of discos and boy friends, to
babies and tranquillised boredom. She had hit upon a
way of letting them see the dismal nature of their future
for themselves. That was where her 'comics' lesson
came in. Most of the girls only read comics like *Blue
Jeans* and *Oh Boy*. She decided to let them analyse
these and compare them, for instance, with boys'
comics.

It was a Friday morning, a good day, nine o'clock.
She was ready to launch out on her theme, show them
the light, lead them from captivity.

She stood before them in one of her 1920s black
crêpe suits, a turquoise silk blouse and black tights.
They stared back at her, wondering at her outfit. Their
pretty faces took everything in. The comics lay strewn
about the formica-topped tables. She had brought a big
pile of them. The would have liked to start reading on
their own and forget about everything else. Some

admired the perfection of their nail varnish. Here and there a mirror popped out and slim beringed hands patted pink curls or touched an earring. Most had four of five studs implanted in each ear. Their throats were criss-crossed with a fine tracery of gold and silver chains and small crosses.

'Can't you see what's happening? Look, these boys' comics are all about boys doing things – adventure. Look at the girls', they're passive, all this stuff about love. Love, what's that? Their lives are simply geared to catching a boy – and what then? What after that? What happens for the next forty years, eh?'

There was a silence and then suddenly from the sweet, passive ranks something began to emerge.

'It's not true! What you're saying isn't true – we don't want to hear. You're old, that's why you're saying it!'

Sue felt shocked. Blood rushed up into her ivory complexion. What on earth was this – a sign, at last, that they were coming alive. She was on the one hand exhilarated by having stirred them up in their heavy passivity, but on the other she was taken aback by the violence of their reaction and their image of her as some fuddy-duddy old schoolmistress. She hadn't thought of herself like that at all.

'But don't you see –' she pleaded, leaning forward so that her long glass earrings caught the light and flashed dazzlingly. 'Like 'er earrings,' one girl muttered to another. 'Don't you see, you aren't living – you aren't finding who you are and what you can do. You might be good at all sorts of things you've never tried. Instead of waiting for "Mr Right", you could be having your own adventures –'

'But we want love! You want to take all the fun out of everything – we don't want to hear.'

They were agitated. 'We want to have fun – if you

21

don't have a good time now then it's too late. I mean, by the time you're nineteen you're old, aren't you, and it's finished – you get married and have kids and then you've had your life.' The sayings of a girl called Pat. She had tropical cheeks and a crimson mouth and blue and white wings round her eyes and her hair was a pale cinnamon confection, a bit like candy-floss only a shade deeper in colour. She was joined by Debbie, a lovely strawberry blonde with porcelain cheeks and a hint of rose on the cheek bones.

'I like to read love stories – it's romance. . . . People like you are too old for romance –'

Sue, geriatric at thirty-four, looking at them, felt obscurely irritated. 'You're proving my point, don't you see? Life should just be starting at nineteen. Why has it got to be over? It's not about romance – what you call romance is sheer exploitation.'

'Exploi what?'

The row raged back and forth, interlaced by the big words LOVE and ROMANCE. They were huge, burning words, Sue thought, and they made her very cross – breaking-pots cross.

It was a relief to be stomping downstairs at the end of the hour with *Blue Jeans* and *My Boy* spilling out from under her arms and the *Beano* and *Dandy* falling to the floor. She was assisted by passing plumbing and bricklaying apprentices who stooped to retrieve them for her and thrust them back into her hands.

Fuming and giggling at the same time, she made her way into the work-room. Like everything else it was slowly falling to bits. Normally on wet days they had a bucket to catch the deluge from the ceiling. There were usual irritations like handles off drawers so that you couldn't open them, broken duplicating machines – one didn't bother with those any more, of course.

22

In the same exasperation she switched on the electric kettle, went to fetch her mug from the locker and dumped the comics on her working surface. Trying to work in there was like sitting in the middle of a draughty corridor or in one of the tunnels leading down to a London tube station. She searched for a spoon, couldn't find one and made a rough estimation of the amount of Nescafé needed and then shook it into her mug.

The work-room happened to be empty. She leaned back at a reckless angle on her hard wooden-seated chair, propping her feet up on the small radiator under the work-bench and began to make herself a roll-up. Of course one ought to give up smoking. She had devised a general studies project called 'Healthy Living' with which she scared classes rigid with the details of heart attacks and how these might be avoided by a diet high in bran and low in saturated fats. Usually at the end of the Healthy Living project some wistful voice would pipe up, 'But what is there left to eat then? I suppose we'll have to give up eating altogether – everything's polluted.'

She told them to stop smoking, cut down on booze and step up the exercise. Whilst she was involved with this, she limited her smokes to quick drags in the work-room where the students couldn't see her. One day, she had decided, she must give up. That day, however, had not yet arrived.

She inhaled deeply, and swung back. Her toes were warming delightfully. Before her eyes danced the frosted globules. The window side of the work-room was completely covered by what Sue thought of as lavatory glass. It let in a cold, opal light but meant that you could see nothing outside whatsoever. Here and there her colleagues had stuck posters with cryptic words appearing beneath pictures of gorrillas or hippos – why those particular creatures, she didn't know. Ted Smales had sticky-taped 'Desiderata' to the patch just above his nose. You needed its advice in there.

Whilst she sipped her coffee, she reflected that she missed Hamish Dean in a way she hadn't thought possible. He had sat beside her at the work-bench for about six years. It had been a very easy relationship. Sometimes she had thought that basically Hamish was like herself. They had looked fairly similar – very tall, slim, dark. He used to pop into her place on his morning off, she'd screw him and towards one, he would arrive at college in time to make himself a coffee before his one-thirty class. There had been a tenderness about him which she had enjoyed. She remembered little things – the coldness of his body as he slipped in beside her in her warm bed. Often, though, they had never reached the bedroom. Yes, she had always had the comfort of Hamish. It had all been running along steadily until his wife had decided to renege on her previous decision which had been in favour of an open marriage. By that time he had begun to murmur about divorce and Sue hadn't fancied that at all. She hadn't wanted the responsibility of him – and it would have been a responsibility. He was the type who pads silently on suede shoes with crêpe soles and invariably wears an old suede jacket. This jacket had once been smart but years previously one of the pockets had been half-ripped off and it had continued to hang in that way ever since. For Sue that pocket became symbolic of Hamish. He would need propping up. In him there was a lack of impetus. He didn't like teaching in the college. Well, he had been able to appreciate the finer points of sixteen-year-old hairdressers or general caterers – but the married

24

women in their thirties and forties had filled him with dread. 'They're so earnest – they know where they're going.' Whereas Sue had found those classes of older women exciting and much richer than the hour spent trying either to enliven or to dampen down the bored sixteen-year-olds.

Once Hamish had launched himself on the divorce theme, she had hastily backed out, and then he had decided after fifteen years' teaching and having gained no sort of promotion, he wanted to escape. He went ethnic and began making pots. So that was it. He left and together with his wife bought a cottage with some land in the depth of the country. This of course meant that they could no longer glance at each other along that strip of formica and thereby make known their need to be lying naked amid furs and silks in her tart's bedroom (she called it her 'tart's boudoir' privately). Her room was indeed a place to titillate the senses. She burnt incense and had beads depending from the mirrors on the dressing-table. These mirrors were set in curly frames so ornate that they verged on the ugly. Strategically placed were marble statues, copies of Grecian men with splendidly symmetrical bodies, heads poised and hands supported on nonchalantly sloping hips – what calves, what thighs, pure lozenges of muscle! Most of these treasures had come at some time from the Rainbow Palace and were Linda's finds.

As though expecting to find him still there, or just arrived, Sue turned and looked down the working-surface. Goodbye, Hamish! Bye bye, tender, mournful Hamish, who would not kiss her. Why not? She had never known, and had held it against him. She had considered it a lack of fire and warmth – ah well – but then when she considered all the males she knew, she found few would could match her female acquaintanceship for depth, warmth, passion . . . she didn't know the words to use.

How the work-room faces changed! Contemporaneous with Hamish and overlapping, had been Harry Drake. At one time she had sat between them and screwed both, but they had not realized it. Harry, like Hamish, had languished on failing to gain promotion, though he had also been falling into a decline on account of his lack of success with his literary efforts. Once, years before, he had had a short story published in an Arts Council selection. From then onwards he had presumed that he would join the literati and become established. It hadn't happened. He would bang into the work-room, setting the notices aflutter on every notice-board in the place. That always meant he had suffered a rejection. He had taken every rejection-slip as a personal insult. They didn't want him. He was being turned down. In the years to come, long after his death, his genius would be recognized. Actually Sue had thought his work quite good, not breathtaking but pleasant enough. He had written her sonnets and been anxious to bed her. Sue had telephoned his wife, Mabel, whom she'd known fairly well. 'Mabel, would you mind if I screwed Harry?' 'No, no, go ahead!' So she had. His odes had been better than the bedroom scenes. They tended to be wet-whimpers, which she had tolerated through goodnaturedness. She hadn't wanted to upset Harry more then he was already.

Finally Harry had turned very bitter and their relationship had culminated in some awful hate sessions. He was convinced that the CIA were having him watched and his telephone bugged – and then he began experiencing panic-attacks in front of his classes. Sometimes he was so drunk he could only hiccup and stagger about and Esme Cartwright, an iron lady who took charge of arrangements at examination times, had accused him of lurching into the exam hall in a paralytic state. She frog-marched him out.

Following close on that episode, he had flung himself into a disused dock and had been rescued by a passer-by. He ended up in the loony-bin having ECT. Now he had left the college. Mabel and he had parted company and he had returned to his mother in Swindon. So his chair too was empty. The college wasn't re-appointing staff if somebody left.

When Harry had been off work for six months before they compulsorily retired him at forty, they'd sent Jim Dacre to fill in for him – so there she was with the young Geordie sitting next to her at the work-bench. He'd had something. It was a certain indefinable aura, the thing she'd thought she'd glimpsed in Gary, but hadn't really. He'd been a man-of-the-people type, had attended an adult college, and had come up as a working-class lad who'd become dissatisfied with being an electrician. His weary, humorous face had charmed her from the start. He wrinkled his forehead when he was talking to you and was very tense and sincere and he'd got light-grey eyes which were somehow a surprise. He'd only reached to her shoulder just about, and his body had been little and wiry. She'd wanted to know him instantly, find out all about him. He'd been married, but his wife and child hadn't come with him as the job was only temporary. Sue had gathered that he and his wife were undergoing some sort of crisis.

Being aloof like a cat, she passed through mood sequences which shifted with the waxing and waning of her obsessions. She kept away from him, but sometimes they'd find their elbows touching along the formica and they'd grin. Talk had run on petty annoyances which

27

hedged them about. He had been quite without pretensions and subterfuge. He'd often prefaced his remarks with 'I'll tell you straight up', and she'd found herself half-mesmerized by the lines on his forehead and the warm, humorous way he had. Yes, he had been very sexy, one of those people who are naturally so.

Shortly after that, she left the work-room, taught three more classes and then decided it was time she set off on the trek back home, calling on the way at various shops to select things for her evening meal. She always enjoyed that. Sometimes it was a pork chop, or a piece of haddock, and then she would buy a quarter of button mushrooms and a small cauliflower, whatever took her fancy.

The first thing she did on arriving at her house was to fill the kettle and plug it in. Over her first mug of tea she read her *Guardian* and relaxed. Whilst she was so engaged the door-bell rang. She heard Cordelia's three swift blasts and then she was in the room. Sue wondered idly what she wanted. There was on her face that winning, innocent expression which meant she was out to involve you in something highly dubious. Weakening, because of course she invariably did, Sue fetched a mug and poured her a fill of tea. There was obviously subversion afoot.

Chapter 4

Cordelia felt that she had been growing up for a hundred years. School wasn't too bad, well, they'd become adept at twagging. A number of afternoons they simply disappeared. Mrs Billington would be grunting wearily on about *Pride and Prejudice* or the imperfect tense in French or it might be a Geometry lesson and they – Cordelia, Debbie and Christine – would be out in the town wandering through the big shops. Their favourite haunts were stores like Miss Selfridge where they tried on glittering jackets, the new mini, sequined blouses and ruffled shirts. Cordelia's great delight was to stand before a long mirror, setting one hat on her head after another and then turning from side to side, raising her hand to the hat and posing as though she were some wealthy lady on the deck of the *QE2* staring out to sea.

They dreamed of the delights of the wealthy. Cordelia fancied white Rolls Royces (though perhaps she'd make do with a Jag), and French perfume and real leather shoes and furs, perhaps a great pure white fur stole which would nest about her shoulders. She admired fabulous women like the dead Monroe.

But there was also another side to her. She

29

sometimes thought she would have liked to have known about black people. Her father had vanished when she was a baby and her mother didn't speak of him. Her mother, she often felt, was like history itself. She had been through so many phases and experienced so much that she had become a great and amorphous mass, which defied interpretation. Why she had taken up with him, where she had met him and why she had in the end dispensed with him, Cordelia had no idea.

The Careers' Counselling from Mrs Barton was basically a waste of time.

'Now, Cordelia, what were you thinking of doing? Nursing perhaps?'

Nursing, impossible! You couldn't really say to Mrs Barton, 'Well, I want to be very rich, wicked, dreadful, rich!' You had to pretend that you had no naughty instincts, that you were ready to do nice ordinary things like being a shop assistant, or working in a factory. To that end they had been taken on a number of visits and had stood watching women and girls in white overalls and with their heads bandaged in white turbans staring stonily at toffees as they trickled along conveyor-belts or gently filtered onto the floor. The toffee, like some immense log had been thudding over and over on a machine which had elongated it – that had been quite interesting – but as for the rest, it was enough to make you fall asleep or else bite your nails.

Then there had been the idea of secretarial work. Cordelia hadn't allowed herself to be shunted into the technical stream, though efforts had been made to force her into it. As you were in the 'C' Stream, what Mrs Barton called 'non-academic', secretarial studies would be ideal for you. She'd say it with a big smile and do a bit of mummying to make you feel that even though she thought you were a bone-head she

30

respected your right to breathe. 'We mustn't let *them* feel they're second-class citizens.'

Cordelia hadn't wanted to spend her days in an office. Well, what about shop work? Though here there had been some hesitation. How many black, brown, chocolate, café-au-lait faces did you see behind counters in shops in that town? None. Such nig-nogs as there were must remain discreetly hidden behind packing cases in factories. Cordelia had got the idea all right, and so when faced with the prospect of what they all referred to as 'The Careers', she would prepare herself to grin from ear to ear. She knew that Mrs Barton would say, 'She's such a *nice* girl, Cordelia Peach, so funny – always smiling. Not very bright of course – but I mean that's not everything, is it?'

When she was at home Cordelia would act both parts for her mother and Tom, her brother, or for Sue. Tom would laugh until it seemed he'd snap in half. Now he was her hero. He was milky-brown and had dyed his hair blond and he walked very slowly with his shoulders thrown back, and most of the time he wore a 1920s fur coat and a long drop in one ear. He moved like a gigantic cat. Tom had style, there was no doubt about it. At eighteen he was running his own band. He played the guitar and sang in a soft sludgy voice and the girls on the front rows would be practically swooning.

No, Cordelia felt that there was absolutely nobody to touch him – and when she was taking off Mrs Barton, he would capture the role and say in a finicky light-coloured voice, 'Cordelia, dear, what about a nice job sweeping up behind the scenes in Woolworths?' The 'Woolworths' issued so sweetly that it was like a caress, or a kiss or a mouthful of chocolate ice-cream.

Sometimes she would go into Ron and Freddy's with him. They lived two doors down. Their house was bewitching as they went in for big gilt mirrors and velvet sofas. A reproduction of Michaelangelo's 'Adam', blown up very large, was in the hallway, reposing on some plum and gold embossed wallpaper which felt soft to the touch like moss. Their front-room was all shades of blue and there were gold cushions and brass coffee sets and inlaid Eastern tables – and Ron liked incense.

Tom really fitted in there and they would sit and look at him admiringly and he'd turn his big black eyes on them and jiggle his thighs up and down. He was always drumming and humming and simply couldn't keep still. She knew he had once thought he'd like to be a ballet dancer but it hadn't come to anything.

It was a funny business having this black side that you knew nothing about. She'd tried to discuss it with Tom but he'd just shrugged and broken into a drumming sequence on the nearest piece of furniture. He wasn't one to talk. It didn't interest him. For him talking was extraneous.

Ron and Freddy came pretty high on Cordelia's favourite list, too, because they were gentle. Freddy would just sit and smile enigmatically whilst Ron lay back in his reclining armchair recovering from his exhausting day and sipping sherry from one of his cut glasses. Sometimes Cordelia would practise the action of lounging on sofas, glass in hand. Sofas were very necessary pieces of furniture. Sue had about five, and in her own home there were literally dozens because it was virtually like an extension of the Emporium.

Through various channels, one being Freddy, Cordelia had heard about the local conservation group, 'Aid' and she had started attending its gatherings in the company of whoever could be press-ganged into going along. At an Aid meeting she had heard of the

32

beautiful tiled fireplace which was about to be dismantled in a derelict house not so very far from where she lived. Who would go with her to save it? She didn't bother telling her mother. She was too busy anyway. Tom had an engagement to sing at a club with his group, so it would have to be Sue.

As Cordelia slipped round the front of Sue's house from her own next door, she reflected that she had in a sense got junk in her blood, and old things. Few new articles ever really had dazzle.

'Hi, Sue, spare a minute?'

'Tea?'

'Please. Anything to eat?'

'Okay. Chocolate digestives?'

'Wow, we *never* have those!'

'They're expensive, that's why not.'

'You mean only take one!'

They grinned at each other. Sue was always planning events for them both. Cordelia had been to the 'Little Theatre' with her quite a few times. On the last occasion they had seen a play about women ambulance-drivers in the First World War. It had made her feel quite weepy, though she'd hidden it, when one of them had been killed whilst driving her ambulance. Cordelia found those theatre trips with Sue very disturbing. They set her dreaming for ages afterwards. She was excited by the sound of the words and the way the tension mounted and the sudden glimpse you got into the way other people lived and felt.

Sue was almost as familiar to her as her mother. She was pretty tough. Cordelia remembered the night when she'd missed the bus from the school disco and hadn't got home before midnight and half-way back on foot she had seen those two familiar figures striding towards her, four-square Mum, with her frizzed hair flying in the wind, like some prophetess, and Sue – six-foot Sue – marching beside her. They had been very cross and her mother wouldn't speak. She hadn't uttered a word until they'd entered Sue's house and Sue had made tea and handed out roll-ups, and then she'd broken out into waves of abuse, saying she could have been raped, murdered, disembowelled, the lot!

'Well, I thought you'd got other things on your mind?' Sue's query brought her back to the present.

'I have.' Cordelia began pleating the folds of a blue velvet smock made from an old curtain which she was wearing over some stretch jeans. She broke into 'I'm the dangerous highwayman!', an Adam Ant number, and snapped her fingers vigorously.

'And what might that be?'

'An adventure.'

'Go on, go on . . .' Sue inhaled her roll-up and kept balancing a tattered slipper on the end of her big toe.

'Well, there's this fireplace. . . . I know exactly where it is – and it wants saving – I mean, you could have it in here, if you wanted . . . or we could . . . or –'

'And?'

'It just means getting it, that's all.'

'I see. And how are we going to do that?'

'Simple. We take a crow-bar – Mum's got a couple – a sledge-hammer and spade. . . . I'll ride the cart down there and we can put the pieces in it and bring it back. Fireplaces are dead easy to fetch out, you know they are.'

'Mm.'

'Well?' Cordelia had already risen and was wandering about the kitchen, touching magazines, books, the Art Nouveau leaded-lights, the fish plates.

'What you mean is, you want us to go this evening?'

'That's right.' Cordelia gave the brilliant smile

34

reserved usually only for Mrs Barton at the Careers. Her face looked soft, immensely self-satisfied and also devilishly witchy.

'Okay, I supposed it had to be. I was actually going to mark Argumentative Essay 7. Saved, saved. I knew as soon as I saw you that you were up to no good.'

'There's nothing to it –' Cordelia said, once more stroking the folds of her smock with long brown hands. 'Look, I'll just whip next door and get the gear and then I'll be back. Mum won't notice – she's gone to one of her anti-nuclear yak sessions.'

'All right.'

Sue fought feelings of faint disquiet as she put on an old kagool that somebody had once left, and wound a long blue-knitted scarf round her throat. She had knitted it during one of her knitting phases. Once that particular obsession had left her, she had no means of re-kindling it.

As she waited for Cordelia's return, she thought of the bodies they were sure to discover in the derelict property. Fairly frequently a column in the local paper would report how some man or woman believed to have been sleeping rough had been found in an unoccupied house beneath a pile of newspapers. Already she saw herself and Cordelia in a police cell accused of murder. All sorts of things were happening at the moment – arson, countless robberies, which took place even in day-light, and numerous rapes. People might return from work to find their houses cleared out and nobody had noticed anything suspicious. Every evening the paper devoted a column to the latest burglaries: where the thief had struck, and what had been stolen.

Sue's gloomy thoughts were interrupted by the appearance of Cordelia.

'Ready? I'll bike on in front!'

They set off down the windy street, Cordelia riding Linda's bike with the cart attached, and Sue walking slightly behind. Their houses formed part of a continuous yellow-brick terrace. At one point a few years earlier the area had become very seedy. What had changed it however, to some degree, had been the demolition of the French convent school opposite. That fine grey-stone building had hidden behind a screen of elms and some spiky railings like assegais. In its place twenty or thirty smart town houses had been constructed. They had open-plan lawns front and back and were neat and boxy and fairly prestigious. The inhabitants of the old terrace began perking up their property a bit, but there was still about it a certain dereliction. The little grassed-in strips by the front door-steps were grimy and filled with dirty paper and empty bottles tossed in by passers-by. And yet there was a feeling of community about that place – you could pop into quite a few of the houses and have a chat if you felt so inclined.

They passed groups of leather-clad youths from time to time, moving in a directionless fashion. Under the sodium lighting their faces shone cheesily. Their hair was short and they often wore a single gold earring. Their boots scraped the tarmac. At the sight of Sue and Cordelia they set up a howling. Sue cringed inside and felt afraid. She couldn't bear physical threats. It was bad enough at the swimming-baths when huge beefy males would insist on bombing into the water, just missing you by centimetres. Cordelia on the other hand seemed quite unperturbed. In the middle of the cat-calling she put up her fingers in a V sign and bellowed, 'Up yours!'

Soon they were passing under bare plane trees. On

the other side of the road a Chinese take-away and an Indian take-away were both squares of orange light and now and then a person would leave, carefully carrying foil-covered containers of rice and sauce. The newsagents, the washing-machine repair shop, Oxfam and the 'New to You' second-hand clothes shop were all closed but their windows remained lit so as to deter thieves.

Their destination was a huge grey brick house which faced onto the main road leading into town. The way in was through a back street. Sue, gazing across at the house in the moonlight, traced shivers of apprehension passing over her back and her armpits itched. Cordelia felt hot with excitement. The garden lay before them, a wilderness of bare brambles, which coiled and twined like barbed wire. A willow towered up, casting a weird black shadow over the convolutions of old gas cookers, mattresses and rusting bed-springs which poked up from the dried-out winter-dead bracken and garden escapes. Before the house were the remains of a patio up to which led a flight of broken stone steps. Sue imagined the businessman's family who had probably lived there, walking to and fro in their long, pale dresses, staring down the garden in the dusk and yearning for something which was bound to happen but in fact never did. They were no different really from the hairdressing apprentices, she registered with impatience, nevertheless the beauty of the ruined house and garden touched her in some way which she couldn't dismiss.

Armed with a bicycle lamp, Cordelia was already at the top of the steps and was trying the doors of the French windows which had been boarded up.

'If you – er, if the cops come – run for it,' Cordelia whispered. Sue felt she was sinking deeper into something which was definitely illegal. She ought to have taken a firmer stand and restrained Cordelia – she, the Further Education College lecturer, should have been keeping the sixteen-year-old out of trouble, guarding her from such bizarre adventures. Somehow she couldn't: for one thing she deplored the waste caused by the demolition and abandonment of such splendid old houses and for another there was prevalent that feeling that amid the tinsel of modern life you must hold onto something from the past in order not to be suffocated by vulgarity and tasteless-ness. Was it that? Was it something quite different? There was really a most extraordinary feeling abroad at the moment – it was as though in spite of, or because of, the drab nature of their existence people were finding all manner of intriguing diversions and new ways of doing things. It was unsettling and stimulating.

She hastily brushed these considerations aside as she followed Cordelia, turning once to glimpse the decayed beauty of the garden: it seemed to possess a mystery and an ugly loveliness such as she had often seen in the industrial landscapes surrounding the town. Docks lay bare and stagnant, grass grew between flags and on bricked wharves, warehouses presented austere pocked faces, barges lay rotting, there were twirls of rusting metal. . . . Somehow it was all in her head as she climbed over broken bricks and through a side door which Cordelia had located.

How ghostly it was! Cordelia shone the torch round the hall-way. They saw a splendid staircase with serpentine coils. The floor was covered with shards of broken glass. Lofty ceilings boasted plaster-mouldings and ceiling-roses. They rambled through big, silent rooms with Cordelia spraying the darkness with her bicycle lamp. They had left the crow-bar and the other tools in the cart outside. This was to be a preliminary scouting expedition.

Gingerly they went up the staircase. Soon they were on the side of the house facing the main road and the rooms were lit up by livid orange streaks from the sodium lamps outside. Every now and then a lorry would thunder by and for a few seconds a search-light would play over ancient flowered wall-paper, piles of old newspapers, cardboard boxes and heaps of useless tat. A cracked, handleless cup, an empty Harpic container had been left as a kind of shorthand for somebody's life.

Sue's nerves were on edge. She felt that at the slightest sound, she would scream. You couldn't know what might be lying under the piles of old rags and the newspapers. The place reeked of damp and urine. They continued to stumble over broken crockery, tin mugs, detergent bottles. There were a couple of cracked sinks, a u-bend for a drain and always slivers of glass, giving off diamond sparkles in the shifting beams of the passing lights.

It was when they were about to return downstairs that they located the fireplace in the last upper room. Cordelia shone the torch. There it was, one of Robinson's beauties with red-tiled surrounds and yellow tulips blooming on them.

'That's brass!' Cordelia exclaimed, scratching at the metal hood piece which was scrolled with languid flowers. 'Wait till Mum sees what we've got – it's gorgeous!'

Even Sue felt oddly stirred, there in the darkness, peering at the find. The stalks of the tulips were long, twining greenish threads, none of the tiles had been cracked.

'We'll never get it out,' she muttered.

'Course we will. I'll belt down and get the gear –'

'I'd better come with you.'

They set off along the landing, stumbling and pattering over pieces of broken brick and glass. Every sound seemed to be magnified so that it rang loudly. Just then Cordelia stopped. 'Shush, something's going on –'

They stood still. Down below them they could distinctly hear footsteps. Sue's heart hammered, violently. She remembered her 'Healthy Living' lessons and the causes of a cardiac arrest. She stifled an impulse to scream. What was often called bravery in battle situations was probably only the individual's desire not to appear foolish. After all, if she yelled it would seem particularly absurd. In the blackness of the stairway she could only see the whites of Cordelia's eyes shining. Cordelia had switched off the bicycle lamp. Sue fell back on her ten years' teaching. 'Better not make any noise. Just wait, they might leave –'

'Kick 'em in the balls!' Cordelia growled.

The steps were crossing the hall-way below.

'For Christ's sake put the lamp on!' Sue commanded. Cordelia obeyed. She shone the lamp straight down onto a man who was mounting the stairs. Surely now the heart attack must come. She expected to feel a searing pain in the centre of her breast-bone. She clutched the banister, rooted to the spot.

'An' what do you think you're getting up to?' the thick-set, middle-aged man enquired.

'I could ask you the same thing.' Sue seemed to have found her voice all of a sudden. Two other figures had joined the first man. They looked very dubious.

'You're trespassing. You can be arrested for it you know, police cells and all –'

Cordelia knew about that – she and her mother had

40

once been apprehended looking over an old derelict warehouse.

'I bet you're not allowed in here either.'

'Look –' the man was addressing his remarks to Cordelia, '– you stop being cheeky and get out of here. I've took your crow-bar and the rest.'

'You what?'

'Oh yes – and if you don't scoot quick I'll 'phone the police and tell 'em I found you in here. We've got permission –'

'Look, Mr –'

'I know your lot, see, know your mother. You tell her you met Mr Brocklesby. Did she put you up to this?'

Cordelia was taken aback. 'No.'

'If you want the tools you can come round to my place for 'em. Now scoot!'

Sue experienced a powerful rush of fury, but remembering that she had declared himself a pacifist and a 'Ban the Bomber', she thought it would be best to withdraw. Cordelia seemed to have other ideas.

'No, better leave it,' Sue said fearfully, putting a restraining hand on her arm. Cordelia accompanied her but muttering imprecations and banging her feet. The men carried on up. They had clearly come for the fireplace.

They found the cart still where they had parked it, but the tools had gone. Round the corner they saw the Jaguar.

'That's his.' Cordelia went over, took a lipstick out of the purse hanging round her neck and scrawled across the windscreen, 'Prick'.

'We shouldn't have left him. . . . I ought to slash his tyres.'

'No,' Sue was quite firm, 'that's going too far. That's criminal damage or whatever they call it.'

Cordelia was fuming as she rode along. Sue merely felt relieved. At least they were still alive and had neither been assaulted nor suffered a heart-attack.

Chapter 5

It was a Saturday morning. Sue generally slept late then, but something disturbed her on this particular day. She thought that she could hear the phone ringing down below in the bowels of the house. Usually she wondered whether or not to bother answering it, and would decide not, turn over and doze off again until midday. This was one of the luxuries of living alone: you rose when you felt like it, went to bed when you were tired, ate at odd hours and took nobody but yourself into account.

This time however she experienced a curiously uneasy sensation in the pit of her stomach. Better go and see. She struggled into her black satin kimono with the dragons snarling on its back and rushed downstairs into the sitting-room.

'Hello? Hello, hm – what? You mean . . . okay, right – I'll be there this afternoon.'

Reeling under the news, she went into her kitchen and plugged in the kettle. Her fingers groped for her tobacco tin. She tried to make a roll-up. What now? Suddenly she saw Linda's face at the window. Linda generally dropped in for a few minutes before she went to open the Emporium.

'Linda, my Mum's just rung to say Dad's had a heart-attack. . . . I'll have to go now – I can't take it in.'

'Poor lass, here, let's make the tea.' Linda set about finding tea-bags, pouring in the water and then providing Sue with a roll-up, because she seemed to be too paralysed to act.

'You see, he always seemed so strong, like a bloody colossus, and he looked after himself – you know, golf, watched his weight – and he's only in his late fifties –'

'Here, take it easy!' Linda handed her a mug. She was her usual unflappable self, the one which had cruised through three marriages and was even now getting the details mixed up. It had all been fairly diverting. 'You'll need to pack some gear then, stay overnight –'

'Yes, yes, I expect Mum'll be pretty devastated.'

An hour later Sue was installed on the train to Sheffield, with a canvas bag beside her on the floor. She had chosen a 1920s squirrel coat to wear over her black suit and tights, and boots completed the sombre outfit.

All the way there she sat staring out of the window, thinking about her parents. They had been annoyed and irritated by the fact that after university she hadn't found a nice young man, married and settled down. Her constant succession of men-friends had disconcerted them. She heard her father saying, 'Don't you think you're a bit old for the jeans-thing? I can't bear to hear your legs scratching together in them.' They didn't like her tat-shop finds and her penchant for 1920s clothes either.

What struggles she had had! Sue remembered the far distant era when she had been Daddy's little girl. He had adored her when she was about eight with her curls and her big eyes. Later, once the boyfriends had

44

started, he had begun to change. Mini skirts had driven him into a fury. 'They're indecent – open provocation.' Her talk of women's groups had angered him too. 'It's all so unnecessary – your mother . . .

He was a self-made businessman and had done very well as an agent for various firms. His mind was geared to figures and profits and insurances. She realised that he had rarely allowed himself to relax from this money-making preoccupation, which seemed so pointless to her.

As the train drew in, Sue caught a glimpse of her mother. They were said to be very alike. She was tall and spare and had big aquamarine eyes. Her hair was short and dyed brown and curled conventionally about her face. Sue always thought that her mother didn't dare enough. Now her expression was dull with shock.

They embraced. Sue felt suddenly that their roles were reversed: she had become the stronger, the sustainer.

Together they crossed the bridge linking one set of platforms with another. It was just as it had always been, checked with bill-boards announcing 'Pregnancy Testing', travel agencies and cutlery firms, and with the inevitable dark-grey dust which she remembered so clearly from childhood. The announcer's voice echoed in the vault. 'The twelve forty-five train from Birmingham will be arriving . . .'

'He's in the Infirmary,' Mrs Edwards said.

'Are we going there straightaway, then?'

'Yes, I think we'd better. I've let Elliot know and he'll be here by this evening, latest I should think.'

'How did it happen?'

'He just didn't feel very well. . . . You know, Sue –' Mary Edwards turned confidingly to her daughter, 'it's not like you expect at all. I mean, when other people

45

say "heart-attack", you somehow think you'll know. It's not like that – it didn't occur to me – and then when your Dad sort of collapsed and had this dreadful pain, I thought it must be –'

They climbed into her mother's shining, navy-blue mini and negotiated new roundabouts and traffic islands. The city had changed vastly over the last fifteen or so years, its boundaries had expanded, and its centre now seemed all concrete fly-overs and curling, whirling swoops of road, hedged by towering biscuit-coloured shops. The little places had been swept away. But increasingly of late the edges of the newness were growing battered and spotted with hard use: shoddy materials and bad workmanship were showing through.

He was lying in a bed in the Intensive Care Unit and behind him was a battery of equipment and dials charting the functioning of his organs. His naked chest was covered with a series of monitors, and tubes protruded from his arms. The first impression was that he had aged immeasurably in a very short space of time, and had shrunk.

Sue fought to hide her shock. She knew that her mother must be struggling similarly. On no account must he see their despair. All he could do was nod at them and speak in a very low voice, not much above a whisper. From time to time he drifted into sleep. After an hour or so sitting by his bed, they left.

On the drive to the Edwards' semi-detached brick villa in a good residential suburb, they said very little. Mary left the car on the steep drive-way. Spring was beginning to soften the contours of the meticulously tidy garden. Its long, sloping lawn was bowling-green smooth, no irregularity spoiling the neat demarcation between lawn and border.

This was the businessman's belt. Successful solicitors

46

and doctors also inhabited it and nearby was the local golf course. It had been removed as far as possible from the pollution of the factories. Derbyshire beckoned a mere twenty minutes' car-ride away, with rambles over the protected countryside.

'I'll put the kettle on,' Mary Edwards said as she slid her key into the lock. 'It's been so strange since he went –'

'Yes.'

They'd only been in the house a few minutes when they heard Elliot's car drive up. Sue hadn't seen him for a long time. As children they had been very close. It had been a teasing relationship. She had egged him on to be naughty, doing things like kicking the ball into Mrs Lacey's orchard as an excuse to sneak in there and steal apples and pears, pinching dried fruit from the pantry and chocolate biscuits from the tin on the top shelf. Once they'd broken a pane in the neighbour's conservatory with a tennis ball. It had felt like the end of the world.

When Elliot had gone away to university to read law, the intimacy had snapped. They had become polite strangers, and of course after his marriage to Pam that distance had increased. Pam was pretty, pert and domineering. She had produced a child, Flora, who was spoiled and yet repressed. On no account must she dirty her dress or create disorder with her toys. Pam hated any of them to visit her: they caused mess. She was simply tortured by changes in pattern.

He was wearing a navy-blue pin-stripe suit and a dark tie. 'Mum,' he exclaimed, giving her a hug. 'How is he?'

'Bad, I'm afraid.'

They sat in the lounge with its chintz sofas and highly polished, reproduction Queen Anne-legged coffee tables. Everywhere bits of china and cut glass rested and the surfaces gleamed uniformly. A Vermeer reproduction hung over the gas fire. There was, of course, an oblong mirror set in a gilt frame.

Tea was sipped from rose-sprigged china cups and there were chocolate biscuits wrapped in foil lying in a cut-glass bowl, which had been an anniversary present. The Edwards observed anniversaries punctiliously.

'We'll all go back later on,' Mrs Edwards said, eyeing her daughter who was sprawling on a sofa in her black suit. Strange black suede boots encased her feet and ankles and then came her long black legs – she looked like some painting, Mrs. Edwards thought, particularly with all that mass of dyed hair. Elliot, sitting beside her, was holding his cup with delicate fingers. He had pale, sensitive hands; all of him impressed with its well-groomed affluence. She felt very proud of him and yet oddly tentative, as though she no longer knew him.

'How're Pam and Flora?'

'Fine, fine.'

They talked families and then went back over the disaster and speculated on what would happen to John Edwards. Sue found the change disturbing. Her father had always been there: her life might heave about wildly but Dad continued with his irritations and his prejudices and his laments about the worsening economy and the coming of anarchy. She had smarted under it, seen his chauvinism clearly, realised that her mother had long ago capitulated, in fact knew no other way . . . and yet now, the alternative, what was it?

'It's so strange without your Dad,' Mary Edwards said for the umpteenth time. She seemed, in her good, undistinguished clothes, to be typical of so many other women. She wouldn't say anything jarring or give way to unrestrained emotion of any sort, and yet she was searching about for a way expressing the awful sense of loss. 'I mean –' she turned her diamond-cluster engagement ring round absently, 'well, it gives you such a shock – and I'm not used . . . not –' She wanted to tell those two confident looking people, her children, that after all these years of never having been alone or having made any sort of important decision, she didn't really know what she could do or where she was heading. She was also puzzled in a certain way because the appearance of things had shifted subtly. For instance, Sue had been a constant worry to her: the fact of her failing to marry, her curious mode of dressing, her friends, her whole life-style had made her uneasy; they had challenged her ways, her values. She had taken certain things for granted, and one was that you got married, a woman who didn't had no status – unless she was perhaps a spinster teacher, but such women of whom there had seemed to a preponderance in her youth, had been a totally different breed from Sue. And children? Well, it looked as though there never would be any. Of course without a husband there couldn't be.

Now, reviewing her own situation it occurred to her that Sue's life seemed more certain than her own. Mary looked at her and wondered what it all meant. And if John died? She couldn't think about it. Elliot was a stranger, somebody whose clothes she didn't recognize, and in whose day-to-day existence she could have no share. How frighteningly quickly they had grown up!

'What have you been doing lately?' she turned to Sue, who then told her about a 'Reclaim the night' march she had been on, and a peaceful demonstration against the stationing of USA missiles in Britain, and then things about someone called Linda who was building up a business, and a 'Women's Rights' group in which she helped.

49

Throughout this Mary smiled and nodded and then poured more tea.

Elliot seemed very nervous. He was smoking heavily, inhaling as though he wanted to consume every tissue of smoke. Now and then his long fingers dusted off any particles of ash. He would survey the lie of his jacket and the lapels as he talked. Yes, Pam was quite well. Laura would be four soon. Of course being so busy he didn't see an awful lot of them. . . . There was an uncomfortable silence. Somehow the absent forth member of the household had held them together because of the antagonism he had inspired. Sue had felt constantly under threat. Elliot had been upbraided for his views on crime and punishment, law and order – most things, in fact, about which John Edwards became irate.

Sue wondered idly if Elliot had changed since his marriage. She hadn't expected him to marry. Mary wanted to hear the dinner cue and realised that nobody would give it. Widowhood. The word sounded a knell. She fought terror and anxiety.

A little while later, they set off once more for the hospital. Things seemed to be exactly as before.

The only time Sue found herself alone with Elliot was when they were waiting outside the Intensive Care Unit for their mother to re-emerge.

'I take it you're thriving?' she chanced, 'you're looking very dapper.'

He heard what he took for mockery. 'No, as a matter of fact I'm not.'

Nothing further was said.

They sat up late drinking cocoa in the lounge and eating toasted tea-cakes, and cheese and biscuits. They were all trying to prevent one another from seeing the extent of their anxiety and grief.

Chapter 6

On that Saturday whilst Sue Edwards was visiting her parents, Linda Peach banged around in her home, getting herself ready for a day at the Emporium. She far preferred the hunting-down of junk to the sales angle.

By about eleven she was pedalling towards the shop with a stiff wind crashing in her face. Seagulls spun up and sailed in the choppy currents. Trade was bad. Very bad. Local dealers were despairing. The laments ran, 'I've taken nothing all day.' Or, 'Seven quid – the entire day, seven quid!' Rumours circulated wildly: Jane's 'Bric-à-Brac' and 'Mrs Thompson's Rare Treasures' were about to close down. The only one who seemed to be thriving was – guess who? Brocklesby, of course. He had recently acquired a huge new furniture van for the transportation of his wares to the docks, or to London. The Scandinavians would give him a good price for his stripped pine. The Germans, like the Americans, favoured big pieces in dark mahogany. And now, of course, there was the sudden interest in tiles.

Linda had felt cross about Cordelia's exploit. Not so much because of her trying to get the fireplace in the first place, but more because she had failed: that really hurt.

'You should have told me,' she'd ranted at her daughter, 'why the deuce didn't you explain? I'd have come as well, we'd have –'

'But you were doing your nuclear whatsit.'

'We could have gone later . . .'

'Then it wouldn't have been there . . .'

Oh well. She'd thrown up her hands in despair.

'What,' Cordelia had persevered relentlessly, 'if we were to nick it back?'

No, that was out of the question unfortunately. They had lost that particular round ignominiously.

Linda was soon opening up. Her plain, parchment-coloured blinds rattled up the windows. She turned round to face the dusty splendour of the Emporium. A corner was dark with assorted furs. Cordelia would always rush in and rub her cheeks on them, murmuring 'Pussy, pussy!' Tom would prance about, trying on the hats until she bawled him out. Her eyes strayed to the assorted flowered chamber-pots and the wash basins and jugs. Some were flower-sprigged, others a charming shade of puce or primrose yellow and white. She even possessed a large, white chamber-pot in the bottom of which was a huge, curved eye like a privet leaf. It seemed to her to be an Eygptian eye outlined in kohl – a mummy's eye. Whenever she was feeling slightly depressed, she would be transposed to a burning hot country where gigantic terracotta coloured figures straddled the landscape and camels wandered, viewing the world throught heavily-lidded eyes. Sometimes she would be almost surprised to hear the bell tinkling and see customers opening the rickety glass door, when she was out there amid the dust and heat wrapped in her burnous. She could feel the

52

flapping of the material, yards and yards of it against her arms and legs – how fluid, how gracious!

Quite a few people strayed into the Emporium clothed in old furs, or ex-army combat camouflage outfits. They assaulted the contents of the shop with a certain determination. When they spoke, their accounts were cultivated of the BBC drawl variety.

'Why don't you run a stall or something up at the uni?' a voice asked.

Linda emerged from her preoccupation for a few seconds to look at the speaker. He was about twenty or so, she supposed, thin-faced and slim. His hair was dyed auburn and geometrically cut. A large gold earring depended from his left ear. He was attired in an interesting selection of garments: an Indian scarf chokered his throat above the collarless grandad shirt; and his thin body was fastened into a narrow black velvet jacket which had lost its pile in many places. But it was his eyes which drew her attention. He had slit eyes, the eyes on the chamber-pot, chamber-pot eyes – Egypt, the Sphinx.

'What?'

'A stall. I mean, if you were to take some of this gear up to the uni, you'd sell masses. . . . It's just by chance that I saw this place, you're off the beaten track.'

He smelt of sandalwood and some other musky perfume. She enjoyed the aura for a while, ruminating. She took her time about answering. If she wanted to make a rejoinder, she would in her way, otherwise she ignored the speaker.

'Hm, when would that be possible?'

'Say, on Wednesday. There's this guy has his books up there then, and there are all sort of things – you know between about twelve and three-ish – when people are having their lunch and wandering about.'

53

'Mm, cig?' she offered her tobacco-tin, which was unusual, a gesture reserved only for friends.

'Don't. Thanks, anyway.'

'Mm.' Linda concentrated on lining her liquorice paper.

'You've got some terrific stuff.'

'You reckon?' Linda sat back in the deep grey-striped armchair, and stared about her kingdom. Her heavy, suet-coloured face gave nothing away.

'Oh yes, I mean these coats, and the pots – Christ, they're beautiful!'

He was leaping about here and there in his split trainers, pouncing first on one thing and then another. 'And these tiles, oh yes –' He had picked up two or three turquoise tiles which were decorated with irises in a deeper shade of turquoise than the background colour.

'I've quite a few tiles that are better than those, in my store. I'll show you if you want but they're at the house –' She warmed slightly to his enthusiasm.

'Brilliant!'

'Look – come back again at five-thirty if you're so keen and I'll take you round.'

He lingered on, rummaging about and finally she gave him a cup of tea. She had a gas ring in the kitchen at the back of the shop.

'Times are bad,' she grunted, as they sat facing each other, flanked by old screens which had been covered with pictures of golden-haired girls and gramophones with trumpets like convolvulus flowers, white thatched-roofed cottages and rows of hollyhocks before them and roses twining over their porches.

Out in the narrow street cars shot past now and then. Depressed women pushed blue and white striped baby-buggies and boys in jeans and leathers elbowed one another. In a row of bay-fronted houses over the way Saturday was jerking and shrieking into momentum – fish and chip dinners if you could afford them, a perambulation up the avenue to do the weekend shopping in the supermarket where trollies clashed dramatically and babies screamed. Linda stared out at it all like some ancient cat who has been washing its moth-eaten fur.

'By the way, the name's Robin.'

'Peach,' she volunteered, without altering the direction of her gaze, 'Linda Peach.'

'Pleased to meet you.' The lad seemed to want to shake hands but Linda ignored his embryonic gesture. It would have been too absurd.

'Would you like me to enquire about the stall for you?'

'Mm, if you think there's a chance.'

They drank their tea and Linda watched the blue and white sky and the shifting shadows on the tarmac and thought how the lad definitely had chamber-pot eyes. They talked in bursts. She grumbled on about the badness of trade and about the recession and unemployment, and he nodded and said yes, she had a good point and was utterly right. He looked so vulnerable in one way that she thought even a light breeze would blow him down. His thin intense face seemed to show everything he felt.

'You drawing SS?'

'Not exactly . . .'

She enquired no further, that was not her business.

'I'm a part-time lavatory-cleaner and attendant,' he volunteered.

'Mm very nice . . .'

'I don't know what on earth I'll ever do, I mean about getting a full-time job, well, there aren't any, are there?'

'No,' her voice sounded flat, 'no, there aren't.'

Finally he pushed off. She watched him springing away on the balls of his feet with his coppered hair standing on end.

After that a few customers found their way in at intervals. A couple of foreign girls began trying on furs and complaining about their price.

'Why, they're practically as expensive as fun furs.'

And Linda had felt almost too disgusted to make a rejoinder as they were so obviously lacking in perception and couldn't even see the startling difference in quality between the old and the new.

She sold a cake-stand and a lacquered glove-box to a teacher who turned up periodically.

Not much else happened and then Cordelia's brown face appeared behind the glass.

'Hi, hi!' she said, doing her usual palm spraying. 'What's new?'

'This kid thinks I should have a stall at the university – and why not?'

'Why not indeed.'

Cordelia wandered off to pose before a full-length mirror, with a beaver-lamb stole round her shoulders. Then she tried on a fox fur. The fox's little face hung down over her shoulder snarling. She executed a tap dance. 'Heigh ho, it's off to work we go!'

'He'll be coming round later to see some tiles – if he turns up.'

'Oh . . . Cordelia took off the fox and went in search of other treasures.

'What you been getting up to this morning then?' Linda asked wearily.

'Things.'

'Like?'

'Nothing much . . .' Cordelia was hauling on a

wrap-over dress with a big black beaded swathe around the hips. It made her look about fifty but was also quite striking. She had a love of things which could make her appear stately and ancient for some reason.

'It's too old for you,' Linda murmured, not really paying attention. She was thinking of a beautiful Victorian lady's chair which she had seen amid a whole lot of junk for Monday's auction at Wainrights. It was in very poor condition – that could easily be reversed. Wainwrights sold garbage and so most respectable dealers didn't even bother to show their faces there.

The total takings for that day were ten pounds. Linda pushed the float and the ten pounds into her canvas bag disgustedly. The light in the street was lemon now, thinning to rose. The young lavatory-cleaner hadn't shown up. He wouldn't, Linda decided, and forgot about him. She continued to sit in an armchair, smoking and surveying the street. On one level she felt quite happy, on another, she was harrassed at the realization of how much a week she must find for her bank-loan – fifty pounds. She saw the figures in her head. They leapt out like speed-restrictions on motorways. Dancing lights turned those into gesticulating gymnasts performing somersaults.

It was almost six o'clock. She finished her roll-up, stubbed it out in a saucer, and looked around for Cordelia.

'Are you still there?'

'Mm.'

'We're off then, girl.'

Cordelia, looking totally improbable in another velvet grandma dress, came slinking out of the back regions. 'Hello,' she gushed in a deep, warm voice. Her lips were big red crescents sliced from an over-ripe tomato. She was Lady Macbeth or some forty-six-hip matron, modelling dressed for the 'larger lady', dresses with a 'more generous cut'. 'Ready, are we?'

'Come on then!' Basically Linda never minded what Cordelia wore. Her only law was that Cordelia must return home at the stipulated time. You could recover from most things, Linda reasoned, but not from being murdered. Cordelia had been reared on the fight-back principle and her mother realised that she was fairly adept.

Linda jerked down the blind and then they left together after locking up. Waiting outside was the young man, Robin.

'Oh er, hello –'

'Why the devil didn't you come in?'

'Well, I didn't want to be a nuisance.'

Muttering at the oddness of people, Linda began to mount her bike and the attached cart creaked in protest.

'Shall you walk back with him?' she asked Cordelia.

'All right. Hi!' Cordelia's huge seal-like body fell into step beside the young man.

The street was empty now. Most people were indoors, closeted in their front rooms viewing Saturday sport on TV or beginning to think of heating up the chip-pan and getting the beefburgers out of the chest freezer.

Linda rode with her head thrown back and her grizzled hair streaming. Perhaps the stall would be a good idea. The air smelt of rotting fish: it was bound to rain. Rain, rain go away, come another washing day. The bike moved rhythmically to the rain, rain and the cart groaned in sympathy, giving voice to the refrain. For a second she got a view into a sitting-room with the tele flashing and a three-piece suite drawn up in front of it and two children sitting, with eyes and mouths wide-open, staring at the screen.

She was back at seventeen and married to Jimmy. It

was during that marriage that she'd won the 'House-wife of the Year' competition. She saw herself slim, blonde, pert, fettling away furiously and whipping up sponges and Yorkshire puddings and cooking all manner of coronary-producing steak and kidney and chicken and leek pies. That liaison had produced Brenda and Tony. Funny to think that Brenda was now thirty-eight, married with two kids and living somewhere in the Birmingham area. Tony, thirty-six, had emigrated to Australia. Brenda had been the reason for her marrying Jimmy. He had been a pint-at-the-pub man and nights out with the lads. Whilst she had been basting the joint and watching the rising of her Yorkshire puddings zealously, he'd been down at the Four in Hand knocking back pints. In a way he'd been quite pleasant, she supposed, except that his views had been incredibly narrow. She'd begun to feel like a mechanical doll.

Basically she had grown bored with being the 'Housewife of the Year'. There had been moments when she had wondered what on earth it was all about. They had occurred mostly when she'd discovered she was pregnant with Tony. Waves of panic had engulfed her. She was being trapped. She'd only just about got Brenda out of nappies and now the whole thing would start again. Of course Jimmy had been delighted: babies proved manhood, and he'd liked them in a sentimental way as long as he didn't have to do any nappy-changing or feeding or looking-after. Little Mrs West, housewife of the year, marvellous routine for creative housework and mothering – everything running like the cornflakes ads on tele, the ones with the gleaming kitchen units and spotless children helping Mummy: no mess, no nastiness, no rages, no impotence.

Linda wheeled her bike and cart up the ten-foot and locked them in the garage. Then she sauntered up the garden path, peering about her. A privet hedge like a forest reared up on both sides. Her garden was a long, rambling strip, in which all manner of chimney pots poked up. They looked like some second Stonehenge or some other ancient sacrificial spot. She had been collecting them for several years. They served instead of statuary for which she had always had a passion. The person whom she admired most in the world had been Barbara Hepworth – not that she'd known her or anything, but then it was often better if you had no personal contact with such people. You could make up all the details yourself and that allowed the personages to remain unequivocally nice.

Automatically Linda plugged in the kettle. Cordelia and the young man, Robin, strolled in through the front-door.

'Phew, what brilliant gear!' he breathed, glancing shyly round at the shadows of great chests, wardrobes, sideboards, tables, chairs, lamps, porcelain. It was in its variety like the shop, only more densely packed with things.

'You want to see some tiles?'

He nodded. She stomped into an adjoining room, beckoning him to follow.

'Hey, they're beautiful.' He wandered from one pile to the next, touching them. Linda could see that he was much impressed. 'You've really gone for all this in a big way.'

'Some sort of way.' She shambled near him, re-acquainting herself with some of the stuff. 'Trouble is, you know, you forget how things look at first – that initial bang wears off. Know what I mean?'

'Yeah.'

'Mind you, in the buying and selling game you can't afford to be too attached, though there are some things I won't part with, like say –'

'Oh hello!' Tom had padded in. He stood in the doorway grinning. The visitor turned to take in the brown-skinned youth with the thick blonded hair.

They all sat round drinking tea, the three Peaches and Robin Layton. Conversation was mostly about the buying and selling of antiques. Robin watched the strange, bulky woman squatting in her deep armchair, smoking and drinking tea. She was a toad, a witch, the shape of her body lost under a series of old coats and jackets. Her feet were thrust into men's black boots. She saw the direction of his gaze and smiled. 'I'm known as the ugliest woman in the world,' she gave out. He smiled too.

It was very cosy in a certain way. Two cats, an orange and a grey-striped, emerged from under some large pieces of furniture and settled down on and around the huge woman. Linda watched the gas fire flaring red and occasionally mauve, and she reflected on how most of the issues about which one might become inflamed weren't really all that significant when viewed in a wider perspective – and yet at the time it would seem that something vital was at stake. Take physical beauty, it didn't matter very much – within a few years, even if you possessed it, soon it had vanished. Yet young girls might spend their entire youth centring on the fatness of their bottoms or their milk-bottle legs, or their lack of breasts . . . quite pointless.

Cordelia was trying to attract her attention. 'Mum, there's the most incredible lamp-post.'

'Where?'

'Down by the old dock – just simply left and they're going to put a new road through there anyway and everything'll be uprooted.'

61

'Hm –' Linda was thoughtful . . . 'Wouldn't mind one for the back-garden. It would look good outside a shop, though, wouldn't it? I mean, if I were ever to get a prime site . . . can you see it?' She gesticulated, seeing her shop, a little one in the centre of the town, painted bottle-green, an old-fashioned place with its own lamp-post standing outside and a window filled with an antique dolls' house, china-headed dolls, tea-sets, and then perhaps white cotton granny nightdresses on old models, pure, erotic, also sullied. Lovely, lovely. Everything in that room had a history, a story. There were so many different intertwining and overlapping threads. Her eyes caught the old brass hand-bell which she used for summoning people to meals or for something important – some teacher would have stood on the steps of a little red-brick 'Board School' (built perhaps in the 1870s), ringing that bell vigorously, a teacher in a smock and with her hair drawn back from her head in a bun. She could have been one of that generation – what was it called, 'the missing generation' – and her fiancé would have been killed in France. And so she had lost her chance and must see her skin withering, her gums receding, her limbs growing rigid, knowing that others no longer saw the joyous girl. Her hands had gripped the handle of that bell, donging out the frustration, the rage which had been consuming her. But that might melt in other moods and become a fierce pride: hadn't she earned her living, kept her life tidy, never been a burden to anybody? Life, a swift, prim adventure.

Linda was recalled to the moment by the other three. She half listened to them, indulgently. Children, she had always felt, ought to be able to discover life empirically. Mothers should not be panting agitatedly on the sidelines, and besides, her energies were occupied elsewhere.

'Do you want to help then – would you?' Cordelia was asking the visitor.

He nodded. 'Yeah, sure, I'll do that –'

'Okay, let's go down there tomorrow afternoon, what do you say?'

'Why not?'

'I'll borrow this van from my mate –' Tom said, he was a planner. 'It's a Leyland – you know a Sherpa. We can prise the lamp-post up and cart it off in that.'

As it looked as though a meal might be appropriate, Linda started burrowing in the cupboards and rooted out some rice. She began slicing onions and flinging green peppers and tomatoes into a heavy-based metal pan. Eating, she always said, should be a joy. She enjoyed food preparation too, throw-back to her 'Housewife of the Year' days. The glossy green of the peppers, the pink-ribbed mushroom umbrellas, their fungoid odour, the tight winter tomatoes, unevenly red (from which oppressed country were they coming, what peasants sweated collecting them?). Then came the garlic press and she squeezed it hard, watching maggots of garlic emerge, to fry with the rice and the rest in olive oil. In went some cold chicken shreds, cardamon and coriander. The savoury contents browned, and into that kaleidoscope of rust browns, russet, sharp green, red, yellow, turning lemon, she poured water so that they could simmer for a while. She fetched out a large bottle of cheap wine.

They settled contentedly about her, half-grown children, cats and the young chap, Robin, who kept watching her under his eyelids. She decided that she would give him four tiles – the ones he had admired the most – and then she reflected how odd life was for a woman, being brought up to think that you only existed so as to be somebody's wife, and then someone's

63

mother – and you might spend your whole life doing the wife number. Sue and she had often discussed it. Of course Sue was different, she had never been dependant in the same way. She'd been a loner and she'd always worked, and her teaching had given her an authority which women who didn't work rarely knew.

Cordelia sat listening to the plotting as to how they would get the old street-lamp, but part of her was somewhere else. She was thinking about the play *Angels of Mercy* which Sue had taken her to see. She remembered the expectancy of the opening minutes when the air had seemed to crackle with tension, as the raw recruit had been talking to the experienced ambulance-driver – and then the way the tension had developed tighter and deeper even, as you got to know what sort of girls and women these were. The death at the end had been like a blow in the stomach.

For a while she could hear the others and then as she gazed out at the ivy-covered wall, something began to form in her head. . . . It was as exciting as the rows of shiny jackets in Miss Selfridge and the gorgeous scents after you'd tested all the trial bottles of perfume in Boots on the backs of your hands – it was a wild, seductive play of voices.

Chapter 7

It was Sue's thirty-fifth birthday. That morning she woke with a feeling which was not easy to define. She ran her toes pleasantly along the edges of the sheet and that was almost as delightful as the sensation of water running out of your ear when you've collected an earful whilst swimming. Your ear is suddenly released from the muffled pressure, there is a pop, and then a delicious hot trickle.

Sue concentrated on the warm edge, working in the crevices of her toes, and idly watched the beaded shades trembling as some lorry caused the house to vibrate. Old Charlie, her favourite statue, was looking quite perky with the early light glinting on his arms and torso. Thirty-five, doom! Half-way to forty. How was it going to feel? For about the last five birthdays she had forgotten for several months after the fateful day, that she had in fact moved on. Some painful jolt would send messages to her reluctant memory, reminding her. Now, thirty-five, and there was absolutely no escape. When she had reached thirty, she had said to herself, 'You're ancient now, girl, over the hump, past it – no need even to bother counting, you might as well trade on being innumerate.' But then somehow a few weeks later she had found that she was still regarding herself as youthful and still resenting the passage of the next year which would work at the destruction of her eternal youth. In this sort of mood it would be easy to return to the jibes of Hairdressers' 1 B. At the time she had dismissed them, but somewhere a barb had caught in the flesh: she was not immune.

As she pulled on her jeans, and a navy-blue T-shirt, and went to wash her face, she braced herself for the day's teaching. The first class was a two-hour English group and she liked that. How was her father? He had not died on that weekend of his coronary arrest but had begun gradually to improve.

Under veils of water, she caught a distant sound of ringing issuing from down below. Cursing, she jammed a towel to her face and took the stairs two at a time, almost losing her balance on the last couple. Her heart hammered. It must be Dad – dead? Another attack?

At last she had the receiver in her hand.

'Yes, hello, yes –'

'Happy birthday, Sue.'

'Oh, Christ, Elliot – what's up?'

'I said happy birthday.'

'Oh, thanks, I thought Dad, you know –'

'Sorry, didn't mean . . . just to say hello –'

'Good of you.'

'And, er, by the way, you might as well know. . . . I've jacked it in with Pam, moved out. . . . I'm living with Simon.'

'Simon?'

'My friend.'

'I see.'

'You might as well know . . . I shall have to tell the parents –'

'Yes, well, I'm very pleased for you.'

66

What did you say? Astounding news, so this was it –
at last Elliot had broken out.

'You'll have to come and see us once we get
ourselves organised.'

'Of course –' After more pleasantries he rang off.

Well, well. Deeply preoccupied. Sue slipped into a
shirt and some matching turquoise earrings. Casually
she ran a hand through a jade bangle and then put on a
black crêpe jacket. It had a bunch of grapes near the
breast area. 'Bluffs,' she murmured to herself, patting
the grapes. Her breasts weren't there, up and down,
straight as a board with a couple of drawing-pins stuck
in it. So what! Simon. Would he be a Greek god? A
nice ex public-schoolboy with good, slightly shabby
clothes? A ballet dancer? This would have to be hidden
from Dad, that was for sure. He'd never stand it. He
seemed to think that anybody whose sexual habits
deviated in anyway from the heterosexual was suffering
from a disease – whereas she had always thought it a
matter of chance whether you chose men or women.

This was certainly going to be an eventful day. Linda
had asked her to come in for a meal after work and she
was looking forward to it.

Stomping through the interconnecting back-streets
on her way to one of the college annexes, she peered
about her. There was the usual line of frenzied drivers,
pushing and horning. Faces behind windscreens
frowned and grimaced. Seagulls balanced in the strong
not-quite-spring breeze. She passed the ghosts of things
– where the railway line had once bisected the main
road on its way to the coast, a red-brick house was
standing beside a brand new, bright brick insurance
office and a William Hill blue and green betting shop.

A short cut took her through a new council estate
which squatted in the middle of nowhere. A man with a

67

crutch fed pigeons every morning at the house on the corner. They would sit in rows on his lawn or on his roof. The people were trying, Sue reflected. They were five minutes from Rosedown and Thompson's factory but they'd planted rose trees and had laid out flower-beds and their window nets shone defiantly white. A gang of unemployed youths on a job creation scheme had painted huge murals on a series of brick buildings facing the houses. They depicted a rural street scene of a hundred years ago: there were horses and carts and butchers' windows with rosy sides of pork hanging up, and a blue sky with clouds like white bolsters and emerald trees, all bunchy with summer leaves. The colours were bold and unambiguous as in primitive paintings.

'I bet it was fun doing that,' she'd said to Tom Peach one day. 'You're jokin' – it would be that painting-with-numbers lark.' 'But even then.' Tom had not been convinced.

In the classroom all sorts of exceptional scenes took place, small revelations, she supposed. You never knew when they were likely to occur. What would happen that day?

They were all waiting for her, fifteen or so people: the two vague rough men with their tattooed forearms and kind bland faces; the six 'pre nurses', pretty, bouncy girls with a mission; the ex-marine engineer who finished all his sentences with 'like'; the handful of unemployed eighteen-year-olds who were stranded with no qualifications and no future. At the back of the room sat the two married women – the blonde one, Marie, with the madonna's face, was the brightest person in the class. She had two children, six and eight, and she wanted to go back to work – but before she could do that, she intended to retrain for nursing. Before marriage she'd been a shop-assistant.

68

'Morning.' Sue dropped her canvas bag on the desk at the front and beamed round. For some reason she found Marie gazing at her in a sorrowful, searching sort of way. She wondered fleetingly why that was, but pressed on. They were preparing to write a short story, which would be part of their course work, and would account for forty per cent of the total marks towards their examination.

'Now let's be hearing about the short stories. Who's got a theme?'

One or two responded. She heard science-fiction fantasies, a love story, and then Marie suddenly broke in.

'I've got my idea.'

'Oh yes?'

'Well, do you remember when we were discussing for and against for that abortion essay? On the next day I was due to go for one –'

Nobody in the room stirred. They were all concentrating on Marie. She had blushed slightly.

'All the time I was listening to the arguments, I was churning it over inside. . . . I'd been convinced that I must have an abortion – I wanted to start a new life, do something myself, you know – and we couldn't really afford my not working anyway . . . and then we'd started talking about murder and how you never know what potential somebody has. It was dreadful. There I was sitting and nobody except me and it knew –'

Sue sat at her desk, leaning forward intently to hear. In one way she felt it was something too intimate to be spoken about, but they were all moved by it and temporarily drawn together, forgetful of themselves.

'Well, and that night I had another nightmare – somebody was murdering me. I'd had quite a few all the same – and then the next day I could't go through with it. When I got to the hospital, I'd said I'd have to cancel it – so I'm having the baby. That's going to be my story. I had to write it. What was odd, you know, was this debate going on all the time – as you were hearing first one side and then the other, I was doing the same inside me.' She laughed softly and looked round at them.

'And now?' Sue asked gently.

'Oh, I'm glad, I'm looking forward to it now –'

'And your nursing?'

'It'll have to be a bit later, won't it?'

'Yes, that's right, a bit later.'

The pre-nurses subsided, whispering and smiling. They were conscious of having witnessed something quite out of the ordinary – but then they were coming up against strange, stirring moments constantly when they went to do their hospital assignments: old people on geriatric wards dying, gratitude for cups of tea, conversations with the terminally ill – you were wrenched out of childhood and into another world without warning. Nothing anybody could say, would prepare you for this. It made the funny side lighter, your delight keener, but the bad became steeper, darker, more impenetrable. The insides of human beings were like primaeval forests. So much they had tried to explain to Sue.

Two hours later they split up for lunch, and Sue strode away from the annexe, taking a short-cut through a little walled garden which was shaded by gigantic elms. Set into the mellow brick perimeter wall were small grey grave-stones. That placid corner had been a Jewish cemetery in times gone by. It was overlooked by a tall red-brick building, the 'Church Army Hostel' which housed homeless men. On sunny days they would huddle on wooden benches, blinking

70

like old cats, watching the students streaming across the gravelled path towards the road – many of them not really old men at all, Sue registered, but giving the appearance of age. Some might have been seven or eight years her junior. She remembered as a child seeing old men shambling out of the smutted portals of the big Salvation Army Hostel in the centre of Sheffield, like ancient tortoises. For some reason they had fascinated her, perhaps because of their imperviousness to the world around them. She admired that sort of egocentricity. Linda possessed it too: she went her own way with wilfulness, would cut her own path and remain undeterred. For women it was much harder than for men because they were generally brought up to value stability and the nebulous word, 'security'.

Over in the main college building Sue joined the comfortable work-room babble. She dumped her books and files on her piece of working-surface. People called 'Happy Birthday', she grinned an acknowledgement. She knew the pattern of the women's lives. There was Elaine, smart, carefully made-up, now in her fifties but looking much younger. She was a widow. After twenty odd years of marriage and six children, her husband had died of a heart-attack. For Sue, Elaine's life was in many respects extremely difficult to understand. Elaine had found her dead husband, Sean, domineering, bad-tempered, downright unpleasant. He had tried to erode her self-confidence by constantly telling her she couldn't do things. And then he had died on her – and by dying he hadn't basically changed anything: he was still there. After the anxiety attacks, the spells of high blood-pressure, it was all beginning to subside – but Sean had in a sense done for her. Why hadn't she left Sean? That was the incomprehensible bit as far as Sue was concerned.

71

Elaine was briskly putting course work into folders. She was always neat, efficient, brittle sometimes, but she was marvellous with students who were undergoing crises. Her sympathy knew no limits, and she would find practical solutions to problems whenever possible.

'Hm, got that organized!' Elaine sighed with satisfaction. 'I want to clear up all the loose ends – I've got to fetch Mother this weekend.'

Mother seemed to be taking over where Sean had left off. Sue went towards the kettle, better make a mug of coffee. Martha was sitting marking, taking no notice of any of them. Martha? She taught full-time, had two young children and returned home to do the cooking, shopping and washing, whilst her husband sat in his armchair waiting for things to be done for him. Sue had made efforts to rally her. 'Why do you think you feel done in all the time? You should make him do something. It really isn't on.' Martha would look hang-dog and nod.

Why did women allow themselves to be door-mats, Sue asked herself as she poured boiling water onto the powered coffee and read the note from the head of department which was pinned above the tea-making equipment. 'If you do not clean up this disgusting mess, I shall take steps to have the kettle disconnected.'

It was like your red electricity-bill on the back of which you would see the reconnection fee set out in bold type. The door-mat question seemed very important on that day, her thirty-fifth birthday. She had never allowed herself to be made into a servant but had fought all the way: domestic issues had formed an ongoing battle with Gary Martin, and with most others too – though the very transience of the relationships had prevented the formation of domestic habits.

Sue bit into a cheese and lettuce sandwich and leaned

back on her chair, dangerously, taking swigs of coffee. She really had never known why women who were financially independent continued to remain with unsatisfactory men. Perhaps it was simply fear which kept them in harness. They had a dread of loneliness and rejection – not realizing that a vacuum automatically fills itself.

Much later, when work was over for the day and she was lying half-collapsed in one of Linda's deep chairs with a glass of white wine in her hand, she decidd to make the announcement.

'I've made my mind up that before I'm past it, I must have a baby.'

The remark was greeted with silence at first. Tom continued drumming on the table and Cordelia, from her position stretched out on the rug, supported by her elbow, regarded Sue curiously. Linda puffed a roll-up and every now and then, the gasp of air being inhaled sounding like an old steam engine coming to rest alongside a railway platform.

'I mean, look, I'm thirty-five – ancient – it'll be too late soon . . . don't think I haven't considered it before: I have. Oh yes, I have –' She couldn't possibly tell them about the frightful scene in which Gary had featured. As she was talking, she suddenly saw Marie's madonna face, 'This debate was going on and on in me all the time, and then I knew I couldn't –'

And now Marie was rounding out, gently growing fuller – what a mystery! She was obsessed by the idea of renewal, the blind, dark workings of the urge, whatever it was inside a woman's body which would drive her to reproduce. She wanted to know that experience, give full rein to her instinctual drives. It would be greater than sex because that was disturbed by the presence of the other person. But this, this would be something quite different.

'Who er – who er –' Linda had become unusually at a loss for words. The rest seemed to imagine that there was a need for delicacy in this matter.

'I don't know, I'll have to think about it.'

'It's not something you should rush into –' Linda's voice was heavy with concern' – the responsibility . . . you can't just, you can't say well, I've tried motherhood – you know it's a once and for all business.'

'Oh yes –' Sue brushed that consideration aside impatiently. She couldn't be bothered with it. But who? Now that was the real problem, to find somebody to donate the sperm.

'When?' Cordelia wanted to know.

'Don't know – it depends on finding the right person.'

How did you go about it? Did you say quite chattily, 'Well, I'm thinking of having a baby, how would you like to be a donor?'

She had talked to her colleague, Tracy Pittaway, who was contemplating having a baby. 'I'll wait until next Christmas I think, till the men are getting drunk . . . you know, some of those really screwed up married types, and then I'll make it with one of those.'

Sue had found the idea repulsive and also underhand: a man had to know quite clearly what was being contemplated, otherwise it would be unfair to him. She had listened feeling quite shocked in a certain way by Tracy's cool plan. Her own idea of the gently swelling bulk and the mysteriousness of the entire birth process was quite different from Tracy's. Tracy had been married and divorced and had a child of six or seven. She bludgeoned her way through life and appeared very powerful, though Sue was inclined to suspect that this was merely a front to cover up her vulnerability. Besides she felt vaguely guilty being so critical of another woman.

74

That night in bed she was conscious of having brought her earlier decision into the open. Like her brother, Elliot, she felt she had broken out. She could discuss it now, dream about it, prepare herself for this new life. When the whole business had first been surfacing during the Gary time, she had been too afraid of it – torn between desire and embarrassment – to have spoken of it to the others, and to have made a conscious admission of her aim. Henceforth things would be different. Linda was only being doubtful because of her own experiences – after all, she had brought up a whole brood of children single-handed most of the time. There was, to keep the balance, Bernie, another colleague, pregnant with her first child. She swelled out marvellously. Her belly had grown like some magic gourd and her breasts had become twin pumpkins. Flowered smocks moulded the magnificent mounds. She called it 'the ultimate fulfilment'. Her baby was due in the early summer. Sue supposed that it was the sight of Bernie and the tranquillity and positive happiness which she radiated, which had stirred her in an unaccustomed way.

Also hidden somewhere at the back of her mind was the memory of that Epstein figure, 'Genesis', in white marble, in a Salford gallery. It was huge and beautiful in its ugliness. Its belly was so monolithic it seemed it would spawn the world, and that day with sunlight glinting on the mound, she had found it so moving that the tears had squeezed up into her eyes. He had captured the essence of creation.

She was still thinking of the broad hands and feet of the statue when she drifted into sleep. She was thirty-five years old.

Chapter 8

After the defeat of the fireplace Cordelia decided that she would fetch the tools back from Brocklesby's house, without telling her mother. She realised that if she let Linda know her plan, she would veto it. So a couple of days after the incident, she looked up his number in the telephone book and as soon as he had answered, she replaced the receiver and then dressed in one of her 1920s wrap-over numbers. Over it she wore a beaver-lamb jacket which made her look like half the side of a bus. She cruised off on her bike with a plastic bag slung over the handlebars, which contained a small quilled hat. She intended to do things properly.

Brocklesby lived in a magnificent red-brick mansion on the outside of which was a big emerald green oblong box with the words 'Burglar Alarm' printed across it. Cordelia had always wondered why people went in for such gadgets – perhaps it was like those notices which said 'Dangerous Dog' or 'Guard Dogs' when in reality there were no dogs patrolling anywhere in the vicinity. Potential intruders were repulsed by an idea.

What a massive place it was! She knew it by sight and had often ridden past on her bike and wondered who lived there and what the rooms would look like. At the side stretched a vast garden on which three of four houses could have stood. So much you could glimpse from the road, if you peered in through the cracks in the big green gate.

Leaving her bike against the wall, she took care to padlock it securely, then she hastily assumed her quilled hat and approached the front door. Her gaze fixed on the bedazzlement of the Art Nouveau stained glass in the porch. Brilliant – what ruby red and pure bright blues!

She rang the bell and waited. Who would come to the door? His wife? Presumably he did have a wife. He seemed to be a mystery man. Cordelia didn't feel she could ask her mother about him because she detested him so much. Well, as long as she could remember he had been enemy number one, the destroyer of the Rainbow Palace – a two-headed monster.

A few seconds elapsed and that seemed ages, and then she saw a figure moving behind the glass and she felt like running away. Why in fact had she come? She didn't really know . . . well of course she had come to collect the tools.

'Hello –' The door was flung open. It was he, Brocklesby, large, rough, and yet overlaid with something else. Their eyes met.

'I've, er, come for the –' Cordelia started.

'Yes.'

It was hard to imagine that this was the hulking figure who had mounted the stairs that evening in the old house – she could scarcely believe it.

'Come in then!' he said impatiently. She looked at his navy-blue back. He was wearing a pin-striped suit. It looked flash. He was flash. Were they enemies, was she going to produce a pistol from her clutch-bag and shoot him in the temples? She might.

He led her into a thickly carpeted room. There was a peculiar atmosphere about it, somehow vulgar and yet not quite. The furniture was very expensive and here and there were ivory chess-sets and jade Buddhas arranged haphazardly on tables: everything betokened opulence. Cordelia liked what she saw, without knowing why.

'Sit down. Drink?'

Now Cordelia didn't really drink, not with any dedication, but the idea of it was pleasing, particularly in expressions like 'drunken orgies' – such things fired the imagination.

'Mm.'

'Whisky, gin, Pernod, sherry?'

The list sounded formidable. She pounced on that last word. Sherry would be the weakest presumably.

He handed her an antique glass which was smeary. It had a longish stem and felt pleasant to the touch. He was staring into her face, wondering about this lumpy brown woman/girl with the big body under the 1920s dress. The crêpe slithered all over and there were gaps revealing areas of plumpness and the quilled hat gleamed and her lips were made up pink and there were bright blue arcs on her lids and above her eyes. She was a bird of paradise – a rare one, very rare. She might be fourteen, she might be ninety.

'Cheers!' Cordelia said, taking a glug of the tawny coloured stuff. People on TV said, 'Cheers!' and on the stage they did too. She raised a hand and flourished an assortment of nails with chipped varnish. He poured himself a small yellow drink.

'Now, I thought I'd better have a word with you. . . . What were you up to in that house?'

Cordelia smiled wickedly at him, 'Same as you.'

He seemed a bit taken-aback. 'Look, I'm a dealer,

you're –'

'Perhaps I'm a dealer as well.'

'Come on, come on, I know your game. If the cops had found you, instead of me catching you, you'd have been in dead trouble.'

'Have you got it then? Did you break any of it?'

He was slightly startled at her interest.

'What's it to you?'

'It was a beauty – and I suppose now you'll ship it to America, won't you?' Her husky voice came on very scornful and her black eyes flashed.

He'd always liked exotic objects. He had to admire her style although she was annoying him. He felt that he was too old and too ruthless to have his actions questioned: people just didn't enquire into his motives, full-stop.

'Not bad, no, it wasn't bad. Seen much better though –'

'Where?'

'Want to see?'

'Yes!' She became all greedy and inquisitive now.

'Come on –'

He led her through a mysterious hall-way which was filled with ticking clocks. They rasped and whirred and there were grandfather clocks with pearl faces and gilt hands of an extraordinary delicacy. Light flamed through the coloured glass door. Cordelia imagined herself to be in the cavern of wicked trolls and giants.

There was a room with a French window letting onto the garden. Outside it was twilight and nothing could be seen distinctly. The fireplace faced them. Its tiles were blue and green iris spikes and the hood was brass and worked with twining stems and bell-like flowers. Cordelia exclaimed involuntarily and he looked slightly mollified.

79

'You like that then?'

'Yeah – the tiles . . . happen to like tiles –'

'What's a girl like you doing?'

She couldn't say, 'I'm at school – and can't wait to quit.' That would have sounded so trivial, such a let-down. He would have written her off as a 'school-kid', finish. Instead, before she knew what she was doing, she'd said the words which meant that now she had committed herself totally. 'Well, actually I'm writing a play.'

'Oh, a play!'

'Yes. . .'

They left it at that for a few minutes, now moving back to the first room. Cordelia swayed experimentally and sipped her drink. He came behind her.

'What's your play about?'

'Things . . .' she said airily, glancing up suddenly under her eyelids.

Brocklesby reflected momentarily that he found her quite diverting. She'd got a matron's body and a face which might have been young.

'How old are you?'

'How old are you?'

'Look, I put the question, didn't I? You was the one I asked. . .'

'How old do you think I am?'

'I haven't a clue.'

'Imagine anything you like – twenty-one, twenty-five. . .'

'You aren't, are you?'

Cordelia squared up her shoulders under the beaver-lamb and the quills on her hat glittered, her eyes gleamed. She was wicked and childish, she gave a deep belly-laugh, showing her strong, white teeth. The sherry slid down her throat. It left a brown-gold taste and made her feel merry, it was creating a good whirly sensation. She would have liked to have danced and sung.

'Why do you have to know about such things?'

'Forget it!'

'I've always wanted to look in this house,' she said boldly.

'Oh well, now you have, haven't you!'

'Yes –'

She said she'd better be going. Somehow he seemed reluctant to let her leave and they started talking about ivory which he collected and he showed her some boxes and figurines and she admired the smooth yellowed faces and the folds in the garments. Her fingers caressed them wonderingly and he noticed the contrast between the brown flesh and the cream of the ivory.

'How did you get here?'

'Bike.'

'You can't carry the gear on it, can you?'

'I can walk and wheel it –'

'No, I'll run the stuff round.'

'Better not.'

'Why not?'

'My Mum wouldn't like it.'

'No, I don't suppose she would.' Old cow, he thought, fucking old cow.

Cordelia felt a traitoress and would have rushed out of the house instantly, but it was the matter of the tools.

'I'll drop you at the end of the street –'

So they piled everything into the boot and she left her bike at his house in a garden shed. She would return for it another day.

'You was the one who wrote that on the wind-screen?'

'Yes,' she said, settling down into the low, soft seat. 'I knew it.'

'You deserved it.'

He turned the ignition key. The even sound of the engine was rich – it made Cordelia think of money and jewels and champagne frothing in wide glasses like you saw in colour supplement adverts. The engine hummed and she felt she was gliding gently through space, she was flying, balanced on cloud billows like continental quilts. As a child she had often fumbled with the window-catch and wanted so much to be able to open the window and fly out over the roof-tops that she had burst out into paroxysms of furious tears at being restrained.

'You're a bad 'un!' he chuckled and looked at her sideways in a peculiar way which made her insides flip like the tail of a giant fish. He smelt of scent and every time he came at all near her, she caught the musky undertones of it and was intrigued.

Now she was busily thinking of how to avoid being seen by her mother. The thought of Linda's anger made her feel vaguely sick. After all they had hated him for so long. . .

'Anywhere here,' she said.

'All right, don't want her to see, eh?'

'That's right.'

'She dun't like me – never has – it's been her own fault . . . that junk place she had –'

'Don't talk to me about it!' Cordelia commanded. 'I'm not the one –' she eased her legs out of the door, thinking how marvellous it would be to make a triumphal exit with skirt gently sliding up and thighs and knees together – the Jaguar look! She hoped some of her friends would have seen her – but then again she prayed they hadn't because word would get round.

82

'You'll come for the bike?'

'Yes,' she said, glancing in at him. He was staring at her body's bigness and thinking how weird she was – bloody dreadful and sexy.

'When?'

'Dunno – when I have time – next week?'

'Saturday, seven-ish?'

'Okay –'

After getting the tools from the boot, she swayed off, wiggling her bottom. The clutch bag under her arm and the tools awkwardly slipping from her hands spoiled her sophisticated exit.

She had other things to think about though: the play, the play? Now there was no earthly possibility of her not writing it. He was bound to ask her how it was going. Besides she wanted to write it.

She dumped the tools in the back shed and progressed through the morass of the back garden, tripping now and then over piles of rusting gear. Nobody seemed to be noticing her arrival up the garden path and she was able to flit in through the kitchen, tip-toe round the banister, and fly upstairs like some escaping cat.

Amid the familiar disorder of her room, she undressed, seeing wedges of herself in the slice of mirror propped up on the wall, as she pulled on her blue-velvet smock and jeans. She was oddly elated. On her table lay two new exercise books and a black biro. She was going to start. Sitting down before the books, she examined them closely. The table faced the garden and it was all dark now. She leaned forward and jerked the curtains to over it. Now she would have to stare at the plain blue cloth. Not bad.

Matter-of factly she pressed back the orange cover of the first exercise book. Good, a margin was printed on the page, that made it look more tidy. It was important for everything to be just right.

The words must be somewhere inside her. She knew what play scripts looked like, because she'd seen them at school. The problem was, though, how to start. . . . Debbie, Mandy, Lynne at school.

Cinderella dressed in yeller went upstairs to kiss a feller. . .

Skipping with a big rope in the yard. Really they're bored stiff. There's nothing to do because they're not supposed to be clever.

MANDY: Let's do something fab!

LYNNE: What? There's nowt–

MANDY: Must be–

Cordelia saw the two girls, the rhythm of their argument, the boredom of their predicament. She sat quite still, struggling in her head for what would come. The rope turning and hitting the play-ground, Mandy jumping in the air.

MANDY: What have we got to look forward to? They're always saying we've got it soft – we haven't no chances, nothing–

LYNNE: My Mam says I'm wasting my life. I'm young, we're supposed to be able to do everything–

Time lost itself mysteriously as Cordelia tried to put the words down. They wouldn't go. It was all stupid and idiotic and she obviously couldn't do it. She didn't know how – and anyway, people who wrote plays were special and they knew lots of things and had masses of 'O' Levels and all sorts of other things. Exasperation made her want to tear up the paper and forget all about it. No, she hadn't ever really said she was writing a play. But she had – it was in front of her. Head down,

84

another try! Then there was a sequence which flowed and she was seeing the school and the classroom and anticipating movements, speaking the fury and irritation aloud. There were funny bits as well, so funny that she rolled about on her chair until the tears streamed down her cheeks.

Sometimes she would feel a dead weight trying to drag her back: the way things ought to be done – how other people, those who *knew*, wrote plays. But she was going to do it her way, as though nobody had ever written before. She remembered the women ambulance drivers and they spurred her on. Four characters had to live, interact – it seemed like juggling: the balls were flying up before her eyes and she had to prevent them from crashing down.

In the end she was interrupted in her efforts because her mother's voice reached her.

'Cordelia, Cordelia!'

'Yeah!' she yelled back.

'Where've you been?'

The door swung open, crashing into the wardrobe. 'Oh, you're here – thought you were out.'

'No –'

'What're you doing?'

'Nothing –' She didn't want to mention anything about the play – if she told anybody else she had the superstitious feeling it would be still-born.

'Supper's ready.'

Usually they didn't have formal meals, but they tended to end up together having something about nine-thirty or ten o'clock.

When they were sitting round the table with their mugs of tea and their beans on toast, Linda announced. 'I'm going to take a selection of gear up to the University to sell to the students. It could be quite lucrative – Wednesdays for starters – we'll have a van, hire one – Tom's going to help me – and Robin.'

'Oh, him.'

'Yes, seems quite a decent sort.'

Sue had just come in from evening class and she and Linda speculated on the gold-mine up at the University, whilst Cordelia continued with Mandy and Lynne. What was it like being young now as opposed to being young twenty years ago? Unemployment now, no cash, American and Russian missiles waiting to clout you round the ears – so many things had been done, conquered. Was there anything left? You had the headmaster pretending to understand, the liberal tendency cloaking the iron fist. You heard people in the fish and chip shop and the supermarket saying, 'What we want is more coppers on the beat – law and order, somebody strong, we need a strong leader to pull us through.' Where were the sixteen-year-olds supposed to go in the evenings? If you met on street corners the cops hounded you. Pubs? They turfed you out – but you'd no money for that anyway. Pictures, two quid a go. Most sat at home before the box and heard about fabulous people with fitted kitchens and Jags and handsome lovers or beautiful mistresses – whatever it was it had to be extreme and interesting. The spotlight was trained in that particular area. If you weren't glued to the box, then you were droning round the estates on your Yamaha waiting for some eighteen-year-old cop to get you.

This was like some entrancing game, where you could interpret life for yourself and at the same time explore lots of other possibilities which you had never known.

As Cordelia sat drinking her tea absently, the world moved before her like one of those globes which the geography teacher rotated: they were magic – only the teacher touched them – the whole world was there, all the infinite variety of sensations. But would you be brave enough? Would you settle for less than a great big chunk of it? She had the secret of the strange man in the big lush house inside her too – her experience, her cut-offness. He was quite different from the lads she knew with their motor-bikes and their jeans-clad thighs. He was battle-scarred.

She was so excited by it all that she didn't think she would be able to sleep – if you slept you were wasting time!

Chapter 9

There were murders in the offing. Sue could sense all manner of ugly hints. That afternoon there had been a meeting of the Academic Board. Their departmental representative, Erwin, had just come hot-foot back, his face wild with impending disaster.

'The department as such will be finished, I'm telling you. . .' His fore-finger smote the air, his eyes blazed.

The rest stood in loose knots sipping their powdered coffee with its half-submerged lumps of powdered milk floating in it. Sue adroitly speared a gobbet with her nail-file as she listened.

'. . .eight hundred sixteen- to nineteen-year-olds are coming through these portals next September – and who's going to teach them? Do you know? Guess! Us! And what about our 'O' and 'A' Levels? Finished. You know what we'll be teaching? Basic literacy.'

Sue, perched on the working-surface, her face cupped in her hands, stared past Erwin. Elaine puffed a low-tar cigarette urgently, her forehead drawn up into tight corrugations. Martha, who had been sitting marking, half-turned her chair. Three male members of the department nodded glumly.

'The end,' Elaine said. 'You need to be twenty-one

and dead fit to teach such groups full-time. I wish I could get early retirement –'

They, approximately fifteen or so of them, were the old guard, the ones who unlike Hamish and Harry had kept plodding on, despite zero promotion prospects and worsening working conditions. Was there an alternative?

Sue remembered how several years previously she'd done a master's degree by taking a year's unpaid leave of absence and eking out enough to live on by giving evening classes. That had been to improve her promotion prospects, but it hadn't – not one jot! Each time a Lecturer II post had been advertised at their college, she had applied, but to no avail: they had appointed outsiders every time, or one of the internal male applicants. She had been filled with fury and had threatened to drag the head of department before the Equal Opportunities Commission – but it had all died down, as things invariably did there.

The men had thought she was a fool, some of the women considered she was fussing over nothing. She had been accused of being 'ambitious'. 'And why not?' she'd come back at them. After that, for months on end, she'd banged around in a rage and been so angry she could scarcely hide her irritation and desire to strike out at something or somebody.

This frustration in her case had been sublimated: she wouldn't go ethnic, or retire to a mental hospital, or consume tranquillisers – she would find new ways – and that had brought her to the house. Now she owned property – and it was going to lead her to the baby.

She wanted more than anything else to become pregnant – she dreamed of it incessantly. On the previous night she had found herself in a white-walled room with curtained cubicles about her, a nurse asking

89

her for her urine sample. 'Have you got your sample, dear?' She had been confused and afraid. Where had she put it? What had happened to it? That morning when she woke she discovered that the sheets were sopping wet with urine. She had sat up horrified and yet strangely moved.

Now as she sat in her jeans and silk shirt, seeming to listen to Erwin and the rest, she was remembering that dream: the feel of her enormous belly and the anxiety of having lost the sample – and then the incontinence, a return to childhood terrors.

But who, who was to be the donor? She found herself going through so many photographs, each accompanied by the owner's drawbacks and assets.

'If we don't fight this, we're finished!' Erwin stated.

'But how can we?'

'Local MPs, contact them . . .'

'It won't do any good.'

'If that's your attitude, might as well just go . . .'

'There's no unity . . . no . . .'

They were all talking at once now. Just then the door at the bottom of the work-room swung open and, surprisingly, in walked Hamish Dean.

'Look who it isn't!'

'Hey, Hamish, what are you doing?' Ted Smales moved forward to clap him on the shoulder. He had broadened, Sue noticed and his hair had turned a pleasing brindled shade: he was two years her senior.

Over the heads of the others their eyes met. Sue registered with a shock that she really had missed him and did like him very much. Since Gary she had been celibate.

'No, I was in town selling pots and I thought, why not come to see you folks, hear the news –' He smiled gently and his steel-rimmed spectacles flashed.

'Making money, are you, lad?'

'Not much.'

'Going to the dogs here, oh yes –'

They came at him with their misery – they were all grey-faced and slack. The term seemed to have been dragging on for ever with its petty annoyances of cold rooms and electricians re-wiring whilst you were trying to teach, and internecine strife, the head of department retiring home with mysterious pains all over him, heads of other departments dying suddenly of cardiac arrests. . . . The list hiccupped on . . .

Hamish drew near Sue.

'Hi!' He looked into her face. 'What's been happening to you?'

'My dear, that would take me a long time to relate, but for one thing, I've become a woman of much beautiful property –'

'You don't say!' He gave a short laugh and she found the glint of a gold filling attractive as she always had done in the past.

'I've bought a house and I'm doing it up. I've actually learnt how to plaster and I can make dove-tail joints –'

'Hm. . .' He was gazing at her, his lids half lowered. He had a big nose and gun-metal cheeks and was always a bit sad and weary, like some clown. She did like that. He was standing close to her, but not touching. Their voices kept a coolish distance.

'How are the pots going?'

'Not bad at all. I'm into big-ware – you know, great big bulbous-sided things –' He shaped them in the air with his long-fingered hands which were coarsening now. 'They're not selling too badly.'

'Do you miss this place?'

'I'm the type who always misses what's not there –'

He gave her a special look. 'How about a cup of

91

coffee?' he asked. His hand touched hers very lightly on the working-surface as though by accident.

'Come back to my place if you want. I've finished teaching now.'

'Okay, let's do that.'

They set off in his estate car. Sue hated cars and always had, like she detested all mechanical things – aeroplanes most of all. She felt powerless when she was sitting in them and she loathed their smell, the way they polluted everywhere with that dank, gassy odour. When she was crossing from one annexe to another she used the pedestrian crossings, because she felt those power-mad, staring drivers would run her down. They were bound to.

'I hate cars,' she said, 'they should be banned.'

'Maybe.' He was easy, as he invariably was. You could relax with him. She wondered what he did with his anger. Had he a deep subterranean wells of it, or had he sublimated it in pot-making?

'Look,' she pointed, 'that's it!'

He blinked across at the terrace and then swerved to park on the right.

'You amaze me!' he said. 'I never thought you'd go in for property – I thought you'd stay in your flat for ever and ever.'

'Well, I didn't.'

She threw open the sitting-room door. 'How about that!'

'Phew – quite something! You like male models – nudes. . .'

'Of course.'

She marched from room to room and finally into the kitchen where she spent so much time. It was an Art Nouveau haven. He looked appreciatively about him and then as she was filling the kettle, he came up behind her and slid his hands down the front of her silk shirt. She set the kettle down and gasped. Turning to face him, she put her lips on his. This time she would force him to kiss her, and he did.

'It's been a long time.'

'Yes. . .' She leaned back against the sink, her cheeks slightly pink. He thought she looked like some huge lily, with her tawny hair, striped eyes and alabaster skin. 'It's lucky you came today,' she said, 'almost as though I'd summoned you.'

'Oh yes.'

'Come and sit down – but let me make the coffee first. I've got a proposition to put to you.'

He sat on her cat-whorled sofa and watched her moving about from cooker to working-surface. All the objects in the room bore her stamp, being at once restrained and exotic.

'Here.'

They sat side by side, she half-turned to him. He was wondering when she would let him make love to her. He was remembering the feel of her, her Arabian nights bedroom: her powerful shoulders and a long cream-coloured back and long straight legs. She was all cream and her flesh seemed thick and supple and when she locked her legs round his neck, he felt as though he'd never manage to hang on and he had to count.

'Well?' He stirred the mug slowly, wondering.

'It's like this. . .' She seemed oddly reticent. 'I'm thirty-five – and I've decided I want a baby before it's too late –' A deepening rose spead up her neck and into her cheeks. She wondered if he had any idea what it had cost her.

He didn't say anything, but continued to stir the mug and didn't look at her. Why couldn't he make it easier?

'I'm asking you – would you be the donor? I would of

93

course not expect, or want you to regard yourself as the baby's father. I would carry on alone just the same as usual – I just want a baby if you see what I mean.'

Hamish didn't move. The room seemed very quiet. Sue heard the thunder of a lorry out on the road. It was a very strange feeling. She couldn't understand what had happened. This was not the same day – it had become something different, in a way more intense, but why she couldn't grasp.

Finally when she had begun to feel almost embarrassed, he looked at her.

'Christ, Sue, it's the most tragic irony. Perhaps some people would think it funny – I don't. I can't oblige – I've had a snip. Eve didn't want any more kids, and when you wouldn't make up your mind before I left college, there didn't seem any point. I knew I'd never have any more – and now this. . . . I would have liked to – I would have been honoured.'

He put his hand on her knee. They exchanged a look, and Sue knew that she had never felt so fond of him as in that moment. She was moved so deeply that her eyes filled with tears. Taking his hand she held it tightly. They kissed again, a very long, tender kiss. 'I'm like an old tom-cat now,' he said, 'quieter, the fire's gone.'

She lifted his hand to her mouth and kissed his palm and closed his fingers over the kiss.

'No,' she said, 'not like that.'

What had happened was in a sense more serious than anything they had done before. Neither of them felt in the mood to make love any longer, so they sat on the sofa and chatted, drank coffee and held hands and then at about four, he said he would have to be setting off on the drive back, or Eve would worry.

'I'm glad you came – I'm glad. . . . You'll come again?'

94

He knew that wasn't the sort of question she normally asked. She was asking now because she wanted to put him at ease: she was sorry for him. Basically Sue was very kind, he had always known that.

'I don't come through very often.'

'But you'll visit me?'

They kissed a plump, child's kiss with bunched lips, on the doorstep, and she waved as he drove away in his estate car.

Chapter 10

The lamp-post. It had continued to stand by the old dock, guardian of the wharf. Like some gallows it towered up near a half-ruined brick building facing the estuary.

Tom, Robin and Cordelia drove there one Saturday afternoon in a pick-up owned by someone in Tom's group. They were filled with a sense of excitement. The flat, derelict dock-land area stretched for miles. It was pocked here and there by brick office buildings. A caravan company had once thrived near its entrance and caravans were still squatting there in lines waiting to be towed away. The detritus of human existence littered the scrub-land, mattresses, prams, gas cookers, doors, broken bricks, bottles and empty tins.

The dock itself was drying out and half filled with curious vegetation which grew in clumps among poison-green slime. To the right of them was a breaker's yard, where pieces of ships, car bodies and all manner of iron objects were mounded up to form a rusting pyre. It lent the area a menacing appearance – was the end of civilization being celebrated?

Every now and then a gigantic cleaver was hooking up and compressing the rusty carcasses of cars.

Clanking and grinding sounded across the water. Sunlight frilled in the flapping tide. A good way away a couple of youths were huddled on the wharf fishing.

'There's nobody about.'

'What about those kids?' Robin was more cautious than Tom or Cordelia.

'They won't bother.'

'Have you got the rope?'

'Mm . . .'

It was decided that they should back the pick-up right up to the edge of the wharf, lasso the lamp-post with nylon rope and then attempt to haul it out by driving the pick-up forward. Robin was to drive whilst Tom dug and superintended the pulling up of the lamp-post's base.

It all sounded easy – perfect in fact, provided the base of the lamp-post didn't prove too difficult to drag up.

On that afternoon with the year's first sun warming them, it seemed impossible that they would fail. Tom and Cordelia armed with pick and shovel set about chipping at the base. They felt slippery with sweat, their hands hurt. Cordelia's eyes stung with the wind from the estuary and her throat smarted. Robin revved and tried to inch the pick-up forward. The engine groaned and thrust. The lamp-post continued to defy the vehicle's persistent roar.

'Shit!' Tom bellowed, 'it's not doing anything.'

'Perhaps we should leave it,' Cordelia's eyes played over the flat expanse – the tumbled concrete slabs, piles of broken bricks and henna-red, cast-iron machinery.

'Not after all this!' Tom's nostrils drew still wider. They gaped, liver-coloured caverns spuming forth malice and power. He heaved and struck – sparks flew off the metal, so many minute stars, a bonfire sparkler.

97

The post began to lean. Its base was some browned fang, unwilling to part company from the jaw in which it was set.

'Pull, pull!'

The engine stalled. The afternoon came to them anew in the silence. Water on wood and lumping grey shingles. Slap, again slap, and the smell of the bladderwrack and smoked fish.

Cordelia's chest felt tight. It was as bad as the night in the house with Brocklesby creeping up on them. Her heart clanged. She was enjoying its challenge on one level. On another she was expecting disaster. What if somebody came and saw them? But why should they bother about a derelict lamp-post which the dock-board would most likely dump anyway? She tried to fight down the dread tingling along her shoulder-blades.

'It's moving marginally, I think –' Tom said, 'look there!'

'We ought to give the engine a rest,' Robin had hopped out of the cab and was standing by the brother and sister. He presented an insubstantial figure in his plimsolls and faded fawn jacket. It was the sort of jacket old men wear in summer with panama hats, a dying breed.

Cordelia stepped back to the edge of the wharf and looked into the water. Something horrible was swilling against the rocks. Sunlight glinted on the slippery black and white fur of a dead dog. She shuddered, letting her mouth open in a ghastly grimace, whilst her whole body shook.

Tom had climbed into the cab this time. He revved the engine so that the air rang with it. The lamp-post began to move.

'It's coming – coming –' Cordelia gasped. The

98

pick-up tilted and swayed and it almost looked as though the pressure of the massive cast-iron pillar would crack it open. But it didn't.

Just when success seemed literally inches away the police van drove up. Cordelia was the first to see it. She couldn't stop herself. 'Cops, cops!' she yelled.

The big white van scrunched onto the promontory and disgorged three, huge hairy alsatians. Wolves, Cordelia thought, as she watched them bounding forward amongst the scrub and broken bits of girders. The end, she wrote, as she had so often done in her exercise books, the end. What did you say now? All action ceased.

The dogs snuffled dangerously around them. Cordelia began to giggle. Hounds of Dracula, she thought, fearsome monsters – the end, the end! The three policemen wore flat hats and their faces were not amused.

'What's going on 'ere then? Psst . . . now –' One of the huge monsters slunk back against the navy-blue leg. Cordelia watched them craftily. She could almost feel them disembowelling her.

'Doing?' Tom's eyes rolled in his head like marbles so that the whites showed. Robin was an empty jacket blowing on a washing-line.

'We were just –'

'Just?'

The wind stung their faces. They all turned to look at the giant stalk of the lamp-post.

'We were saving the lamp-post for posterity,' Robin said firmly. They examined him with disbelief. Who were these unlikely people – two negroes and one peculiar white? In some way they felt affronted.

'You are trespassing on Dock Board property – and you are trying to steal.'

The blood-hounds whimpered and shook like some Greek chorus. Cordelia felt an awful giggle urging its way up her throat.

'You'll have to come with us to the station.'

That was it. They drove in procession, slowly, away from the entrancing wilderness of dock-land.

'Do you suppose they'll lock us up?' Robin wanted to know.

'Oh yes,' Cordelia said, airily, 'they're bound to.'

'Shall we escape?'

'Don't be silly, it's an experience!'

'Well,' Robin said, resigned, 'it's one I could do without.'

They spent an hour at the police-station being questioned and were told that they would have to appear in court and would be charged with trespass and attempted felony, then they were allowed to leave.

Linda, being at the Emporium, remained blissfully ignorant of the drama, and Cordelia didn't bother to go round to tell her, instead she rushed to her room, wrapped herself in a long garment made from a velvet curtain and went on with her play.

Let's change the world – change it?

Yes – no, that's quite unnecessary, just a bit a face-lifting.

Mrs Brown's been dead for years. . . . Now gels. . . . gets on her pleated skirt and applies her orange lipstick, been doing that for at least twenty years. What if she didn't catch the 8.15 bus – didn't . . .

Cordelia stared out into the garden, yes, what if, what if you stood everything on end and refused to be fossilised? If you refused to accept what you were taught, how you were taught? She wrote words on a blank sheet of paper and was entranced to see them. Mandy and Lynne were angry. They wanted to do something. Boys weren't enough – they had the same dreams, but they were their dreams – at which you had to serve as some sort of hand-maiden.

Whilst she was struggling and sweating and chewing her biro end, feeling how satisfying it was when her teeth sank into the yielding blue plastic, she was largely unaware of anything else – and then she remembered she was to visit Brocklesby to fetch back the bike.

But how the hell did you write a play? Sometimes it seemed to be going all right and she was playing all the parts.

MANDY: I'm going to earn a million and find out what I want to do, by myself. Nobody'll ever say, you're wasting yourself, again.

LYNNE: I'll be a stripper – the fabulous Lynne Marchant with a diamond in my belly as big as a sugared almond and a blue butterfly tattooed on my midriff – and I'll have a gold g-string and a gold pair of nipple shields – *(Lynne capers to and fro. Fanfare of trumpets – Lynne with carnation in her teeth.)*

Brocklesby would open the door – that house was like Aladdin's cave – ivory chess-sets and statuettes and jade. By, but he was smooth – and rough at the same time and his face leered as though he'd swallowed some noxious brown cough medicine! And he was intriguing because he was quite capable of being diabolical – he was the wolf in sheep's clothing – no, he wasn't, there was nothing of the sheep about him. He was just awful and everybody would be furious if they knew she was prepared to parlez with him – it was letting the side down.

Well, she'd just go and fetch the bike. . . . After that

101

there would be no need. . . . Cordelia disentangled herself from the curtaining and her jeans and sweatshirt and then for a few minutes she posed before the full-length mirror, surveying herself in her dark maroon bra and pants. Her big brown body overflowed the twists of lace and slippery nylon. She fingered herself curiously and then smiled. Soon she was slipping into a floppy rayon 1930s dress – someone would perhaps have worn it to wave off soldiers at railway stations. Cordelia had gone with Sue twice to see a film about the lives of a group of women during the late thirties and forties. She'd loved the wedge-heels, the print dresses with their clumsy virginal sleeves, the big white faces and plummy mouths of the actresses. You couldn't re-create that because you lived in a world on the fringes of punk and it was constrained by moneylessness and a conservative desire to conform.

She walked through an early evening into a stiffish wind. The sky above the just-budding plane trees lining the avenue was the colour of yellow crocuses. Blackbirds called and their voices struck up echoes and Cordelia felt the old excitement turning in her – what a seductive world it was!

Mandy and Lynne were still in her head, waiting to live out their destinies.

She pressed one finger on the white domed bell. It rang in the vaulted interior. Perhaps he wasn't in! Now that would be an anti-climax. She had tried out her guilt and put it aside and hadn't even considered that it might have been a needless exercise.

He came. The door opened. They surveyed each other, or rather she fixed her attention on a place above his left ear.

'Come in!'

102

'I thought perhaps you'd decided to impound my bike –' She looked at him now directly, challengingly.

'Now, would I do that?'

'Yes, yes, you might.'

'Drink?'

'Please.' She swayed into his sitting-room in her print dress and fur.

She amused him as before. He was not a little curious about her. Women in the main couldn't surprise him any more. He had been married and divorced twice and had lived with a number of other women at various times. It had been fairly diverting but he hadn't taken it all that seriously. Human relationships, he had often felt, did not have the substance of property: with bricks and mortar or jade Buddhas you knew where you were. With women – no, a hundred times no! They had wanted to organise him and he would not be organised. He liked his chess set where he had placed it – he didn't want somebody else creasing the pages of his newspaper or speaking to him at breakfast. He cultivated his own routines like some people did gardens.

'What do you want, gin, whisky, Pernod, sherry?'

'Sherry, please.'

'Here.'

'Ta.'

'Now then tell me about that play you're writing.'

Cordelia giggled and her dress drew tightly across her thighs.

'Well, it's about three girls –'

'Go on –'

'They're stuck at school with nothing to do and nobody thinks that anything good's ever going to happen to them.'

'Why not?'

103

Cordelia, as she looked at her sherry and then let her glance take in the room and heard the muted calling of the birds along the avenues, experienced a moment of real enjoyment. The lamp-post affair had been quite exciting – but this, this too was special. 'Well, you see, people say everything's been done, that there'll be a nuclear war, and we'll all die and that'll be that – and the economy's sinking and we won't have Rolls Royces any more –'

'Hey up – I didn't know we all had!' He raised an eye-brow in appreciation.

Cordelia gestured his objections aside impatiently. 'You know what I mean – the potentiality for Rolls Royces – and yes, they're telling you all the time that in their day, there was no this and no that. But now, oh now there's everything!'

'Mm – so you feel you've got your nose pushed out of joint?'

'You could call it that!' Cordelia took a deep drag of sherry and promptly sneezed. The glass dangled precariously from two fingers and her dress was splattered with brown grape-seeds of liquid.

'Allow me!' He leaned across and dabbed at her thigh, and Cordelia approved the adroitness of this operation.

'Thanks,' she grinned and sat back. 'I'm just deciding –' she continued when he had moved back, 'whether to make one of these girls brown.'

'Does that make any difference?'

He really wasn't all that despicable when he looked like that. His huge nose nebbed imposingly and he had a curved mouth, with deeply defined lips. Cordelia was vaguely reminded of the barn owl in the glass-case in Sue's bedroom with its big round gold eyes set into what looked like crochet work. His head was intricately

104

feathered over. Old Brown, Beatrix Potter's dangerously slumbering creation. At any minute Squirrel Nutkin might over-step the mark and end up in Old Brown's pocket.

'I reckon so –' She stretched her legs and twiddled a foot in a 1940s black suede sandal.

'Why?'

She hadn't thought it out in so many words and she wondered now whether she ought even to try to convey any of it to him, because after all, he was the enemy.

'Well,' she hesitated, 'it's that being different bit – you know. . . . I mean, I'd like to know about black people and all that – but there never seems to be a chance. I've always lived around here but when somebody comes, you suddenly notice they're staring at you. They don't think, this is a girl, they think – she's brown. . . . Know what I mean?'

'I'm finding out –' he said comfortably.

'Not that I think about it much. It was different when I first went to primary – and now and then they'll say "nig-nog". Not that I care. Nig-nog, pig – so what?' Cordelia gave a deep laugh and they smiled at each other in complicity.

'Oh and another thing I don't like is the way everything in the shops is the same and people do the same things and there's nothing way-out to surprise you – and things aren't real –'

That had struck a chord in Brocklesby. He leaned towards her.

'Ah, but that's the reason I go for old gear – old gear's different, isn't it?'

'Yeah, you're right. That's why Mum collects, I reckon.'

Now they were back in forbidden territory.

'I'd best be off,' Cordelia said, talking down into her glass. She placed it carefully on the table.

'All right.'

105

They both rose and stood a few feet away from each other.

'Well, right, I'll get the bike, shall I?'

'Yes, come round the back then –'

But somehow when they were standing by the shed where Brocklesby had locked the bike, they still continued to linger.

'Thanks for looking after it.'

'Pleasure.'

'Better go then!'

'Like to come and see us again?'

She could have leapt in the air with relief and bellowed her loveliest vulgar word, when he said that, because she'd thought he wouldn't ask her.

'Yes, when?'

'Next Saturday, same time?'

'I'll do that, bye –'

She waved two fingers at him, wheeled the bicycle through the big green gate and floated off down the avenue, though that meant in reality creaking along heavily. It was all so exciting she was almost going pop.

Chapter 11

One Monday at the start of the Easter holidays Sue was very busy marking the mock 'A' Level examination scripts and hundreds of Comprehension papers which were Course Work Eight, the last piece of continuous assessment work at 'O' Level. She had the comprehension exercises spread out over her big kitchen table when the door-bell rang. 'Shit!' she muttered gloomily through her teeth. It was early evening but she couldn't think about it, nor about anything except the passage about the girl swinging on the chandelier and the confrontation with her headmistress – and then the sheet of Jack Lane's prepared answers, all set out in his spidery handwriting. Award two marks for 'because she was considered. . .'

Had she felt more energetic, she might have argued with Jack about his model answers, but frankly, she felt too drained – teachers invariably complained of tiredness. She banged through to the front-door. Behind the leaded lights she saw a male head. Gary Martin.

'Hi,' he said, smiling, as though she had seen him only the previous day.

'Hello.'

'Aren't you going to ask me in then?'

He was a little more haggard-looking than before but otherwise exactly the same, including the permed, blonded hair, the flier's jacket, the collarless grandad shirt.

As she stood back and let him enter, she knew that it was his beauty which had seduced her before. He still had that Botticelli angel quality. She remembered their meeting in the conservatory. Even as it had been happening, she had been aware of its vigour and beauty: after the initial minutes had passed nothing would ever be the same again. Excitement had been a raw nerve – glass, light shining and green tropical plants, with water gleaming on their thick leaves, the honk and screech of a mynah bird. . . . But it was over. . .

She was afraid suddenly. This was another day and he was a different person, so was she.

'Very nice,' he said, looking round appreciatively, 'you're moving up in the world.'

'You might call it that – I wouldn't. Tea?' she strove to keep her voice cool and indifferent.

'Thought you'd never ask. Well, what's new?' He sat down on her sofa, his thighs wide, grinning at her. She glimpsed his pointed teeth. He had a cruel mouth.

'Lots of things. How's the course going?'

'Okay.'

What was there to say? What had she ever said to him? Now it seemed impossible to find a topic.

She handed him a mug. It had been awful, she remembered. She hadn't wanted to feel jealousy, but it had poisoned her: all the time she would be wondering where he had been, whom he had seduced. The need to know the truth had eaten into her. They had made frenzied love time after time, until he had been almost

108

reeling. Four times in the afternoon, again, again – it had seemed to her that his prick had not been large enough, she could have taken his hand too . . . all of him. Then she had put her lips round him. It hurt her to remember.

The sheets remained spread out on the table and she concentrated her glance on them.

'Busy?'

'Yes,' she said shortly, 'masses to do – it's the busiest time of the year.'

What to say? A sudden freak hail storm clattered on the windows. She looked at the shining ivy. He had taken off his flier's jacket and left it on the arm of the couch. She was uneasy, remembering what they had done together.

'When you were here,' she said in a cold voice, 'I had no fantasy life: you killed it. Now I'm having the richest fantasies imaginable.' She sprawled in an easy chair in her jeans and striped shirt.

'What does that mean?'

'I'm not sure.'

It could have been quite simple but it wasn't. She felt incapable of forgetting the past. He probably thought it was merely a matter of touching her, they would make love – but it wasn't.

She caught herself thinking of Hamish – the ludicrousness of it – the pathos of his turning away. This was even worse and she didn't know why.

'You say some fuckin' queer things but then you always did.'

'So what are you intending to do as a career?'

'Haven't the foggiest.'

'Why did you come back?'

'Just thought I'd drop in – you know, see how the scene was here.'

109

'Yes,' she thought, 'the latest girl's probably got sick of you, there's been a row, so you came back, like you do periodically to see your ex-wife for instance. Screw her and then move on, just on a whim.'

Sue drank up her tea, took an emery-board from the table and began filing her nails, waiting for him to go.

'What's up? You waiting for me to push off, or sommat?'

'Well, you can see I'm busy –'

'I thought you'd have been glad to see me?'

'Did you?'

'Yer –'

'If I hadn't been so busy. . . . I've got a hell of a lot to do just now. You chose the wrong time.'

'Okay.' He stood up, casually pushed his arms into his jacket and rattled the coins in his pocket. She stood up too. Over her shirt she was wearing a long cardigan and she thrust her hands deep into its pockets.

Basically, it had all started with him, she realised. Had he referred to it, she would have found the situation intolerable. On that last occasion they had been split apart because of it. She walked briskly to the front door, striding over the electric lead from her drill, a hammer, a cardboard box.

'See you,' he said and as he turned, his pale face looked hurt. He was staring straight at her.

'Bye.'

She watched him go out to his Yamaha, put on his crash-helmet, kick-start it, climb on and roar off down that straight street, with the wind tugging at any escaping curls and at his flier's jacket.

For a while she stood there. They had been in her bedroom. 'I want a baby – I'm not asking you to do anything but provide the sperm, get that quite clear. . .' 'You must be bloody joking, I'm not falling

110

for that. Look, I can't – I've had enough of kids, I've got two already, haven't I?'

No, he hadn't wanted to. They'd been over it and over it – she assuring him that he wouldn't be expected to assume any paternal role, she actively didn't want him to – and he intent on disappearing as fast as he could.

That was another chapter of her life which was over, quite over.

She plugged the kettle in once more and marched up and down the kitchen. It had unsettled her. Two evenings previously she had seen *The Marriage of Maria Braun* at the Film Theatre. Maria's negro lover had affected her strongly. With infinite tenderness he had lifted up Maria as she had murmured, '*Ich bin guter Hoffnung*', telling him of her pregnancy. That night Sue had dreamed the negro was making love to her. The sweetness of that dream had remained with her throughout the following day and she had been convinced that this big, ageing man with the saggy belly was also in her life. He had stroked her arms, kissed her long and slowly, touched her nipples, running his fingertips in light circles over them, then he had kissed the pinkish brown points and found his way between her legs repeatedly. And this anonymous lover was quite unlike Gary, she saw that now.

As she poured water over the tea-bags, she realised with a shock, Gary had not really been tender and it was this element she craved – tenderness, acceptance, no shrillness, no aggression.

Stirring her tea, she took it to the seat in front of the table and sat down, letting her eyes stray over the marking. She was powerfully moved by the afternoon's indirect revelation. Again her night-time world seemed to come creeping into the room. It was early evening

111

and she could hear the black-birds singing in her garden. She remembered the face on the screen, smiling, the heavy body dancing, swaying from hips and shoulders, pressing her – a dance in a room with palms and white cloths on small tables, a dance which was melancholy, funny, tender, like a clarinet solo.

She was always watching other people's lives – couples to be exact, wanting to know what they gained from being together, what they sacrificed. Gary had accused her from time to time, 'Christ, you're always analysing, there have to be great talk-sessions after even the simplest things – why can't you let 'em rest?'

In the beginning she had thought that somewhere there must be a man with whom she could share everything – someone who would understand. . . . Understand what? The things which were important to her and moved her – but she hadn't discovered that person and knew now that she wouldn't ever. And perhaps it didn't matter anyway.

This was supposed to be a non-smoking time but she couldn't resist fumbling in the table-drawer for her tobacco and cigarette papers. She lined her liquorice paper methodically and then lit up, inhaling deeply. She was simply in no mood to continue marking for a while.

She pulled on a fur jacket and went out into the garden, down the little path and under the rustic arch. It was a cold bright evening and the silver birches trembled in the east wind. She looked at the lawn, the little pool where the green frogs lived, at the green and white shafts of ornamental grass and beyond to the second rose-arch – through there lay her vegetable garden. The rhubarb was pushing up bright pink knobs of stalk and frilly jade leaves were spreading. At one point she'd almost been seduced by the self-sufficiency

112

notion – of retiring to some commune out in the country and living off the land. But she hadn't and wouldn't. She enjoyed teaching – she loved beautiful things – had come now to ownership and the comfort of it. Her roughing-it days were over: she had slummed enough. That was another reason for parting with Gary. He had still to work through slumming and come full circle.

The late sunlight shone whitely on the pool. The ten-foot-high privet hedge rustled. Blackbirds' song pealed in long fragments of melody which the wind bore away. Beyond the wall at the bottom of her garden the old railway track had run, and way off across the road was another terrace of houses with lights beginning to sparkle in their windows.

She was touched by the shiny orange of curtained windows and the bird-song – they spoke of space and loneliness. Not that she was unhappy. . . . Later she would make cheese on toast and tea and get back to the business of marking. She might groan about the ardours of teaching, but she had a job, as she continually reminded herself. The garden pleased her. It represented hours of pleasant pottering about and had nothing to do with the aimlessness which she associated with Gary or Hamish or Harry – they had passed and now had disappeared from her life.

Still no donor of sperm – no one to fling her in the air, and spin her round. . . . 'Mind you,' she thought, smiling, as she turned back indoors, 'they'd have a devil of a job – my being six foot and weighing ten and a half stone! Their little legs would buckle under 'em!'

She thought of Eddie, one of her eighteen-year-old 'A' Level students. He came up to somewhere around her navel but oddly enough she found him very attractive, spots and all. He was square of body, bullet-headed, dour but very bright. Eddie, Eddie, Eddie. They laughed over a private joke. He looked at her, she at him, long slow eye-contact through a class of others who dreamed, dozed, anything but be involved or attend, whilst she snorted and screamed occasionally – but basically concentrated on Eddie, who would perhaps get an 'A'.

Those young men gave her pleasure to watch because their bodies were firm, their necks strong and their movements precise and they were always laughing and grunting at each other. In discussions they talked as though nobody else had ever voiced these arguments before, nobody had thought their thoughts.

Could Eddie be the donor? Eddie – no, not really, that would be too great a responsibility, both for him and for her. She felt vaguely maternal towards Eddie. He was preoccupying her as her knitting phase had done or her Art Nouveau: her explorations were obsessive and continued until she was ready for a new craze.

So Eddie, Eddie, Eddie. . . . She again drew up the chair to the table and gazed at the model answers and thought about the splendid audacity of the schoolgirl in the passage swinging on the chandelier.

Chapter 12

Linda was now taking fur coats, granny nightdresses, chamber-pots, jewellery, 1920s dresses and all manner of exciting and mysterious oddments up to the university on Wednesdays in the lunch hour. There she set out her stall next to that of a second-hand book dealer. She watched the interest flowering on the faces of passing students. They rummaged feverishly, tried things on, bought impulsively.

It was a day out for Linda. She sat on a plastic-covered 'Union' armchair, sipped coffee from a vending machine and puffed her roll-ups, studying the varied types. What she liked about them was their intentness and animation. She sensed they appreciated her goods and that was important to her because she had a special relationship with what she sold – almost a love affair. She could fall for a pair of brilliant orange, red and blue cockerel tea-pots, or a piece of Art Nouveau tapestry with dull maroon tulips twining all over it.

Altogether these sorties up to the university to hold her stall were proving very lucrative, for more worthwhile financially in fact than a day at the shop. Weekdays at the shop could be a waste of time – she might not see a single customer the entire day. Dealers were reaching near panic point and were removing to other towns or closing completely. One reason for the sharp rise in the number of closures was of course that there had been a sudden big rate increase.

Robin had taken to dropping in quite a lot. If he turned up in the afternoon and she happened to be brewing tea, she would offer him a mug and he would settle beside her in a big armchair and drink his tea companionably. She mentioned one afternoon that she was thinking of taking a van full of gear down to Oxford or Cambridge. She was sure such places would appreciate the type of articles she sold.

'Yeah, brilliant, brilliant!' he said, 'shall I come with you?'

'If you think you get your lavs done in time.'

'I reckon Tom might stand in for me –'

'All right then, you're on! I mean to say,' Linda drew thoughtfully on a roll-up which was almost as thin as a match-stick, 'there's that chap, Jenkinson, comes up from London with a furniture van, does the dealers, rakes around and then off he goes. Thinks he can buy cheap here and sell for a massive profit in London – and then there's bloody Brocklesby.' She stamped the roll-up out heavily under the heel of her boot.

Robin sat very still in the chair, watching her. He enjoyed Linda's ballast. After having spent his entire life expecting to die at any second and being generally very nervous, it was a relief to find this immense, solid woman. She was matter-of-fact, stoical, he admired her.

'You don't like Brocklesby?'

'No – he's a shark, and he thinks he's going to dominate this town and little people like me'll get squeezed out. But, we shall see – I'm just starting up

116

. . . once I get my foot properly in –'

They were interrupted by Tom. His yellow wire-wool hair appeared behind the glass and he came breezing in.

'Listen, folks, I've got an idea –' He twirled about a few times and executed a number of ballet-type movements and then came to rest with one hand poised above his head. 'Mind if I use your ladders and binoculars? I can go round looking at roofs – if I spot any missing slates I'll knock on the doors and ask 'em if they want me to put 'em back –'

'Okay, okay, only watch what you're doing on the roofs and don't fall off and don't do my binoculars in. I've got those for bird-watching.'

'You only went once.'

Linda snorted, remembering that disastrous bird-watching episode. She, Cordelia and Tom had been rambling along pleasantly enough one afternoon on the side of the disused dock and she had been peering through her binoculars at what she had thought to be a skylark, twiddling away at the notched wheel between the lenses and getting a decayed brick building and then a wad of cloud, sometimes a lot of frog-spawn swimming hazily, when a heavy voice had sliced her meditations. 'And what would you be doing? This is private property.' Cops of course. And the constable had been very suspicious of the three of them, what with her being the 'ugliest woman in the world' and the two children being chocolate coloured and arrayed in Joseph's many-toned coat. He hadn't been quite able to believe what he was seeing and had sought any old excuse to take them to the police-station. In fact she had tamed him by enquiring about wild life – a few judicious questions and he had been launched. 'Very interested myself – there's reed warblers. . . . I've seen

117

foxes down here, you know –' He had droned on for half an hour, which Linda hadn't minded because some of the stuff was quite interesting, but Tom and Cordelia had been pulling faces behind the cop's back so that she had wanted to crack out laughing.

Tom was never in one spot very long. He danced his fingers in the air and was out of the door, like some Puck, banging it so that the glass shook and the blind twitched.

'Have you always wanted to do this sort of thing?' Robin asked.

'I didn't really understand it was this I wanted. You see if I clearly know what I'm after, I'm determined then. I simply have to do whatever it is,' and then she told him about her tap-dance obsession, and she didn't share that with many people.

She'd come from a big poor family and there hadn't been any trimmings. But some girls she knew had received dancing lessons. She'd seen them tapping rhythmically, heel toe, heel, setting up an exciting syncopation. Their red shoes had flashed, weaving patterns and setting up their own beat. It had caused her to patter her feet in imitation. One day, she'd promised herself, she would tap-dance. And then years later when she'd had her first family, Brenda and Tony, Brenda had gone to dancing lessons and Linda had seen the magic notice. 'Tap for adults'. She'd rushed out and bought a pair of red size six tap-shoes which she couldn't afford.

'Oh, I could hardly wait to get 'em home.' Linda's hand described a magic gesture and the young man watched, spell-bound. 'This box, white shoe box – you know how pristine they are – and I lifted the tissue-paper and it crinkled and there were my massive tap-shoes – red, shiny, beautiful. God, did I tap! I

118

tapped and tapped. I was at this class and they all turned out to be people who'd danced before – so I had to watch how to do it – but I did. And then I'd go home and I'd be tapping whilst I was frying the chips –' Linda rose from her chair and did a few experimental taps. She lurched breathlessly up and down and her eldritch curls flapped, her glasses vibrated.

'You are lucky,' Robin said.

'Why?'

'Doing things. I mean, I tend to think about things very thoroughly and then not to *do* anything. And I think, well, if I did the thing I might be disillusioned. Were – I mean – were you?'

'Oh no.' Linda subsided into her chair. 'I loved that tapping, every minute of it. I'm not one of those people who're more in love with the idea than the reality.'

The young man shifted his feet. He was always seeing feet: feet under loo doors, feet in casuals, feet in suede shoes – sly, creepy, bold, threadbare, aggressive, feet in love. Water gushed and trickled continuously so that he would think of water-meadows and long-ago Sunday walks with Mummy and Daddy and the labrador.

Linda was thinking of a shop which she had seen vacant not far from the station, right in the centre of the town. She imagined how she could set out that window with choice pieces – not the usual stripped pine tables and dressers, there was too much of that around: no, something altogether more imaginative. She'd move in the ceramic water-coolers – three beauties in descending sizes, finely decorated with white flowers and little scrolls and with their brass taps gleaming.

It wasn't simply that she wanted to make money –

or needed to make it for that matter. It was just the challenge and the pleasure of unearthing objects which she found interesting.

Chapter 13

It was the Saturday of the big demo. Sue set out with Cordelia to walk to the point where they would pick up the bus which would take them to the start of the march.

They walked along briskly and Cordelia had to quicken her steps to keep up with Sue's long loping stride. Cordelia was in an excitable state, what with the thought of meeting Brocklesby that evening and then there was her play which seemed to be assuming a life of its own. It formed a counterpoint to what she was supposed to be doing – preparing to take some useless CSE examinations: they'd not deemed her bright enough for the 'O' Level stream. She could see that CSEs were things you did simply to keep you quiet – you had been designated as 'factory fodder'.

Her suede ankle boots made a pleasant padding sound which alternated with a squashy splat where the right sole flapped against the pavement. The play edged along all the time and was her secret – she saw the heroines bludgeoning and charming their way through great stills of time.

Cindereller dressed in yeller, went upstairs to kiss a feller – how many kisses did she give him last night?

How many? Six, seven, and then a tap-dance routine –
tap-dancing in a back-yard with your dreams spinning
high in the sky above the tall orange chimneys and the
check pattern of grey slates and black TV arms.

Sue had her hands screwed into the corners of her
fox-fur jacket. What were they going to see, she
wondered? Crowds of people tended to unnerve her
but she'd felt obliged to be there on that Saturday.
She'd explained it to Cordelia and had given her a new
run down on Cruise missiles and Trident. Cordelia had
listened, smiling slightly as she invariably did. Tom was
busy roofing and besides he said he couldn't care less
whether the world fried to a crisp in a nuclear holocaust
or not. He thought it a waste of time protesting against
an abstraction. He had been quite adamant that he
wouldn't go, much to Sue's annoyance. Her intolerance had increased as his stubbornness had hardened.

Lines of yellow-brick terraces slid by and the avenue
of plane trees and the main road hedged by little shops.
Finally they were sitting on the bus with all the others,
lots and lots of youngsters in jeans and leathers whose
spiky punk hairdos of orange green and pink resembled
sea anemonies or sea urchins. Some like crown birds
had their heads covered in quills. Then there were the
old guard in anoraks and heavy shoes, people who had
experienced two world wars and seen a similar course
of events before.

When they dismounted the placards were assembled
and the crowd formed into a long column. Trade
unionists rubbed shoulders with Quakers and Labour
and SDP supporters. The black letters swayed on the
sheets of paper and canvas. Babies dozed in push-
chairs as they were propelled forward by earnest
parents in blue kagools.

Stuck in the middle of the throng Sue couldn't help

but feel a pang. Here was a feeling of comradeliness and like purpose. The noise of the combined footsteps created a dull thunder. Some people were singing. Once she glimpsed Eddie with three or four others from the same class. He looked straight at her and then away, giving a brief nod. She thought of him for a while. In her celibate existence he loomed like the boys who had obsessed her when she was eighteen. She wondered idly if after a time you forgot about sex. Did you become impervious to it and able to disregard it utterly?

Mile after mile they tramped. Sue thought of old newsreel films of refugees and shots of escaping people in war films: the real and the imagined had become one. No matter however much they would have liked to have avoided it, those murky and dreadful images belonged now to them all and were part of their collective consciousness. They had not been at Buchenwald, nor even been alive at that time but it had joined the archetypal nightmares, the dreams of falling, of suffocation, of being burned alive.

Moving along up front Sue saw Tracy Pittaway, in conversation with Ted Smales. Ted was in Sue's department, quite a likeable chap; fattish, indistinct, he had obsessions just as she did. Currently he was eating sunflower seeds and eschewing butter and diary products. He was forever proferring some grubby paper bag, the contents of which seemed highly dubious. Unlike Sue though he also went in for drastic changes in his style of dressing. He could be a fat parcel in a businessman's suit, or an angry adolescent in jeans and parka, or even an apparition in a long black leather coat, the type beloved of meat-trade apprentices. It would strain round the middle button and hump over his bottom. He was a fervent supporter of conservation

123

and Green Peace movements – and it was he whom Tracy had finally settled upon as the provider: Ted was to produce the sperm. He'd agreed, albeit unenthusiastically. Sue had overheard him saying to Tracy, 'Well, I've got my evening class Tuesday. If I've seen you Monday, should we best leave it for this week?'

Impregnation had not occurred and Tracy was in a distinctly dangerous mood. Ted had withdrawn into vagueness. They both confided in Sue. Tracy took an authoritarian line and Ted complained in a bruised, somewhat offended voice about Tracy's high-handed behaviour.

'Well, I mean – I only did it to help out, didn't I? See what I mean? See, Sue?'

Sue had smiled and said, yes, she did see and never mind, such things had a way of happening. In the beginning she and Ted had been fairly light-hearted about the whole business; she'd winked at him and said, 'Never mind, this is just a trial run so you can get ready for me!' The only thing was she'd realised she couldn't manage anything with Ted – it just wasn't the remotest possibility. He had tried in the past to suggest an amorous relationship but she had laughed it off. They'd even been on a walking holiday together and had rented a cottage but each had slept separately and they had spent a week contentedly like brother and sister. He was interesting because he collected facts and Sue didn't mind hearing about how old bricks were made and what Andrew Marvell did where and how Roman drains worked – but still . . .

The crowd parted a while and Sue saw the stolid set of Ted's back – she wondered which one he was concentrating on, his 'Desiderata' poster or his 'Flora' pattern of fruits and polyunsaturated fats. It was the parka today and not the apprentice meat-trader outfit.

124

Tracy walked with a bounce. Her back was ram-rod straight and her hair vibrated. Sue could imagine the set of her pekinese face and the way her eyes would be bulging. Had Ted been given his cards, she wondered? If he had, he would no doubt be feeling fairly relieved about it.

On they treked – the long march, Sue thought. Cordelia, beside her, was humming to herself. When people were on long marches were they also beset by the swarming of inconsequential thoughts: Tracy and Ted and the grimly serious job of procreation; Eddie, Eddie, spotty, squat, Eddie sitting on the front row and staring whilst she pontificated about George Eliot – because of course one *must* be serious if one was literally exploding inside with a fit of the giggles.

After four hours they reached the big glass college block in front of which the rally was to take place. As they approached and heard the 'No Nukes' band playing and saw the crowds massing, Sue experienced a surge of seriousness. She was rising on a crest of emotion. It lifted her as she looked at the faces around her and away down the length of the ornamental garden opposite the college. The crowd was mainly young, thank God. They were protesting for their lives, their chance to live – why shouldn't they be able to enjoy what life had to offer? The world was theirs too, predominantly theirs, or should be.

People sat down on the pavement edge and slouched, relaxing their shoulders. Sue and Cordelia squatted on a low wall and began to eat tomato sandwichs. Ted Smales smiled and blinked at them and came over to join them.

'Not a bad turn out.'

'No, pretty good.'

Police moved down the length of the road trying to drive the demonstrators into one area. People listened to what the blue uniforms said, nodded vaguely and continued as before. Babies were being fed, toddlers skipped about and tumbled. Thermos flasks were being unearthed and plastic sandwich boxes came out. The music brassed up. Feet tapped. The sun was shining.

At two-thirty prompt the speeches started. First came the local CND organiser who then handed over to one of the town's Labour MPs. He was a little chap with the look of an evangelist. His voice carried well. He spoke about millions spent on defence and cuts in educational provision and welfare benefits. He gave them facts. They heard how the next Labour Government was pledged to scrap Trident.

Sue was flying high, taking off over the glass tooth of the college. Her eyes filled with tears – it was true, all true. She didn't want trees to die and children to be born malformed or not at all, birds to drop dead in the hedgerows. What the hell did wars achieve anyway? She couldn't bear the idea of being responsible for the extermination of millions of Russians – and here was this little chap speaking the truth.

Next came a Trades Council man and then an Anglican priest with a worn, handsome face who talked about love. He leaned forward, engaging their eyes and the wind whipped at his long black clerical vestments. Love, love.

The spectre of Trident and Cruise missiles loomed up – they were names for nasties. She'd read the eye-witness accounts of the day the bombs dropped on Nagasaki and Hiroshima. She could imagine the panic, the screaming, the frightful burns on people's skin, the scabrous patches, the boiling, unassuagable pain. Some of those images were as clear to her as though she had experienced them herself and they had always been so.

She became aware then of Cordelia who was following the speeches with rapt attention.

126

Two hours later the gathering finally dispersed. It was cool now and the street was covered in brown shadow. In the melée Sue found herself beside Eddie. He kept his head down in the obstinate way he had.

'Well?'

'Well . . .' He obviously didn't want to speak.

'Do you feel it was worthwhile?'

'It was okay for us – don't suppose it did any good though, won't change anything.'

'But imagine, Eddie, all over the country other people will have been demonstrating.'

He looked unimpressed. She felt momentarily annoyed – it was so rare to share something with anybody. She had expected him to experience the same euphoria at herself. She supposed he was right, but that didn't change anything, it was as though he had dashed cold water in her face.

When she asked him if he wanted to come back for a drink, surprisingly he said yes. On reaching the house Cordelia cut off abruptly, murmuring that she had something to do.

He moved about the kitchen, staring at things and yet not saying anything. His unease was conveyed to Sue. She brought some lager out of the fridge. He came alive then and concentrated on removing the bottle tops and pouring out the lager, without causing too much head.

Sitting on the sofa he looked like a small, bullet-headed peg-doll. She could have stroked his slicked-back dark hair and dusted him down as a mother did three-year-olds. Yet on another level she was way beyond that, she was still lingering on the flagged court before the college, listening to the MP talking about the decline in the Social Services and the money being squandered on machines of destruction.

They began to talk desultorily about class members and she tried to take it all seriously. Detached she watched his earnest moon face, a small boy's face. He would struggle with Anglo Saxon in future – if he were lucky enough to get a university place and a grant – and imagine himself in love a thousand times, quite predictable. But she had passed through it all before. As yet he was too involved in the importance and seriousness of himself to be able to tell her things. She realised suddenly that she needed to have a prospective lover share fragments of his life with her, otherwise there would be no magic: it wasn't simply a matter then of window-cleaners staring through plate glass passionately at you, like the herculean airman in Badedas adverts as he lopes across the lawn to the naked lady gazing at him from the house.

So it couldn't be just flesh – she'd tried that many times already. And Tracy Pittaway was perhaps finding that out too. 'Come on Ted, now is the hour – the egg is zooming down the fallopian tube. Ready, steady, bang!'

'. . . you get very impatient –' he was saying.

She looked at him as though in surprise. 'Do I . . . well, it's not easy. I mean half of the group are so passive, sometimes I could scream – just in the hope of getting some sort of reaction.' She was surprised at her own fierceness.

He appeared slightly pained. She sensed that he was afraid of her, the weight of what she was, and she could see his point of view – after all experience, thought, feeling, they did accumulate in you like some mighty compost heap. Many men traditionally liked to form teacher relationships with younger women: she felt she had no time for a teacher relationship with a young boy. She wanted resonances, if she wanted anything.

128

But perhaps she had given up. With that she took a deep draught of lager and turned to look at the ivy-covered wall. She was irritated by her own naivety in thinking that things would be so simple.

Another lager later when the sky outside was pale lemon tinged with rose and she would have liked to walk out into her garden and watch the ripples on her pool where mountain-ash flowers fell and left white dusty stars which gradually sank, Eddie started pleating his fingers.

'. . . you know I often think I can't feel anything –'

'Why's that?'

'Well, you see, there's this girl, Trudy, I mean at one time I thought I was fond of her. I was you know, but things change – and then well –' He rubbed his face with his palms, settled and re-settled his thighs uneasily and finally blushed. 'She seems to think we ought to be thinking of setting up together – and she keeps pressing me, you know. . . . She wants me to say I love her and all that – and to give her reassurances. She's sure I'm going to reject her and I want to, but –'

Sue drank the rest of her lager. It was like the time when she'd been knitting the angora and mohair sweater. It had been the last of a long line of knitted beauties. She had knitted every evening and on Saturday afternoons, her needles had clicked, metal and wooden. But then, coming towards the end of the wool and mohair – half way down the second arm to be precise – she had experienced a surge of impatience. Basically she had had enough, she was through: that had been the end of the knitting obsession. The tide had gone out. Then she had turned to her reading of feminist literature. Sometimes she had sat up until three and four in the morning and had slept with the breaking of the dawn.

129

What should she tell little Eddie? He was deeply involved in his own heartlessness and his girlfriend's longings for reassurance. She knew his girlfriend's situation intimately. The only solution was for the girl to turn away – take up badminton, yoga, pottery, in other words seek a diversion, focus her attention elsewhere and leave him to his introspection.

'Well,' she said kindly, 'things have a habit of working themselves out. You'll find that time will solve the problem for you. Look, I'm going to throw you out, Eddie, I've got simply piles of essays to mark –'

Although nothing had been said between them and now wouldn't be, he had a feeling of let-down, as though something had been withdrawn. He rose clumsily.

'Okay, thanks for the booze, see you on Monday.'

'Yes,' she said, striding before him to the front door. The street was quiet and it was a wide spring evening, edged with frostiness. Ring doves called in the old trees behind the house.

He plodded off doggedly down the long strip of pavement and did not turn round. She felt sorry for the girlfriend somewhere who would be expecting Eddie to animate her, to press the electric light-switch which would illuminate everything.

Chapter 14

Cordelia sifted through the muddle of her bedroom, looking for what she wanted to wear – she had a habit of hoarding things. The walls were a patchwork of Toyah, Buck's Fizz, Shakin' Stevens and Adam Ant. There was also Jimmy Hendrix and Elvis – funny to think that they were both dead and she had never known when they were alive, yet somehow she felt she had. Strings of bright beads hung from a hinged mirror, felt-tips, pencils, exercise books drawing paper lay scattered on the floor, and also two or three childhood dolls and a teddy with worn ears, which she still cuddled at night. She couldn't imagine ever giving up Ginger Teddy with the bells in his ears and the shabby bits on his paws and ears.

She struggled into a slithery print dress with square shoulders. The cleavage swooped so low that she drew the material together with a paste brooch.

Then she had a frantic scrabble in a biscuit tin where she kept her make-up. Standing before the mirror she drew in blue wings about her eyes, and outlined them with kohl. Her lips came up like maroon gloxinias. She stroked dark maroon varnish on her nails. There she was – big, brown, oozing, giggling, ready to take on the world.

As she rode off in easy swoops on her bike, with the

beaver coat flapping, she remembered the morning's march. Sometimes she had felt like crying but hadn't known why: it was something to do with it all being so serious – then there'd been the three women from Greenham Common. She imagined that they were probably not much older than she was. They'd spoken about being encamped near the American base in a protest against the forthcoming siting of the Cruise missiles. They said it was expressly a woman's venture because they wanted it to be non-violent and intended that it should remain like that. She'd thought she ought to go and join them – *do* something.

Now her thoughts were turning to Dale Brocklesby. She had dreamed about him, strangely enough. He had caught her wandering in strange rooms, come upon her without her knowing and she had screamed at the sight of him – she was frightened of him. Underneath she was feeling guilty and excited too: she ought not to be going there. Her mother was very tolerant of practically everything and the worst thing she could ever have done, would have been to fraternize with the nasty. . .

She'd told Linda she was going to see Debbie Barratt, her friend from school.

There was something about him – his awfulness and . . . it was that which intrigued her. She knew that lately she'd been growing more and more sly. As her mother said, her left hand didn't know what her right hand was doing. And somehow she couldn't stop. It was like the play. All the time she was torn between enthusiasm and self-doubt. There was this determination driving her on. Sometimes she'd feel herself falling back on bits of time when she'd been about eight or nine – hateful periods. She'd been very big for her age, a fat blob, and nothing she'd ever worn had been like anybody else's – well, it couldn't have been because they'd no money and anyway things wouldn't fit her. She'd needed clothes for a twelve-year-old. The kids at school had made fun – 'Oo, look at 'er, fatty, fat-dabs, fat-dabs, nig-nog, who's a nig-nog, ten little nigger boys!' And she'd been defeated at first and had wept at home secretly, but then she'd watched how Tom had behaved. He gave people a clatter if they tried anything on. He'd been big and square as well and he could do a lot of damage if he was so minded.

Suddenly it came to her what she should do. Lynne would decide that all the big bumper Rolls Royces, diamond and fur dreams would be useless if they didn't do something to prevent a war – so she'd up and off and join the women at Greenham Common in their sit-in. What about Mandy and Debbie?

By the time she'd reached Brocklesby's house, she'd driven herself into her familiar mood of defiant elation.

As before, she rang and waited, admiring the glass in the door.

'Hello,' he said.

She grinned at him, delighted to see him, though she had no idea why.

'Hi.'

'I did wonder whether you'd make it –'

'Look, I said I'd come, didn't I?' Her dark eyes flashed, she gave a husky giggle. They stood together in the hall for a few seconds and she saw the ruby light from the glass falling in bands across his grey hair, What had he seen, done during all those years?

'You might have been scared off.'

'Not me.'

'No?'

'I go out for things and do 'em, I don't dilly-dally. I'm not a cowardy custard.'

133

'Good. Sherry?'

'Mm.'

She sat on the deep plushy sofa as before. Her nostrils widened as she sniffed the room. She looked at the big jade Buddha by the window and the chess set. All these things were him. He always seemed to be in navy-blue and his shoes were expensive black slip-ons. Just watching his feet made waves of hot excitement surge in her middle – though she tried to pretend it wasn't happening and keep it all quite noncholant.

The sherry tasted warm and rich. She wiggled her toes contentedly.

'What have you been getting up to then?'

'Been on a demo today –' and then she told him about it and how she felt she ought to join that band of women.

'That 'ud be a loss,' he said and smiled.

'How do you mean?'

'Try to figure it out, little lady!'

'But aren't you afraid of getting blown to bits?'

'If we do we do.'

'I want to know there'll be other people coming after me.' Cordelia thought she sounded like Sue, because those were the things Sue said.

'Have you ever thought that perhaps God wants the world to come to an end? How can you say what's the right thing?'

'It can't be. Anyway – you tell me what you've been doing?'

She heard about an auction he'd been to in the south somewhere. Would she like to see the carpet?

He led her upstairs and she followed. Presently he flung open the door of a room which was packed with all manner of costly pieces of furniture, mahogany bracket-footed desks, windsor chairs, rosewood

134

occasional tables, Bergère suites. The Persian carpet suggested some Eastern boudoir with its maroon and royal-blue and purple tones. It made Cordelia think of gold and blue peacocks with a million eyes, of dark-skinned men whose mournful black eyes longed for paradise.

'Like it?'

'Brilliant! Are you going to sell it?'

'Eventually.'

'I don't know how you can.'

They were standing side by side in the doorway, looking into the room.

He suddenly put his arm round her shoulders. She experienced an electric shock. It seemed as though she might whirl off the edge of the world – the world was surely flat – she was spinning, rocketing out into the blue out yonder. Very deliberately he traced the tips of his fingers down her cheek. It was exquisitely tantalising. But he did no more than that. He looked into her face, focusing a strange and concentrated gaze on her. She was dazzled by his unknown places – all those crevices – the pain, the laughter, the diabolical side. He was powerful. He grafted, he had concrete goals and made his mark – but he had another puzzling side which she couldn't fathom. Nothing stopped him.

Was this the same man she had encountered on the stairs in the house during the fireplace escapade? She was intrigued by the way everything seemed to be slipping away – was brilliant, so thrilling her heart seemed it would stop.

'Come on,' he said. She didn't want to come on, but of course she did.

'What about the old play then?' he asked once they'd made it back to the sitting-room. Cordelia's nerves were in a state of suspense, trembling and yet taut as stretched wires – what she called 'dithery'. Anything at all might happen – but then again it might not.

'I'm having a struggle,' she said truthfully. 'It's very hard work and sometimes I think I'm no good at all if you see what I mean.'

He looked at her thoughtfully, having resumed his former seat.

'You have to keep going though, it's the only way. I've seen it myself – with the business – if you want something, you have to get it and never be put off.' He thought how young she seemed. It was something to do with the slimness of her neck and her big trusting eyes.

'I've got things I want to say, you know, like what it's like being –' she paused, aware that she'd almost given the game away.

'Yes?'

'Sixteen.'

'I see.'

'I've told you the rest – you know, people doing all sorts of things, just to keep going – like our Tom doing roofs. He was looking up to see if there were any slates missing – got Mum's binoculars and this cop came up later and said he'd had a complaint that Tom was peeping at this woman in a bedroom – and he said to the cop. 'What did I see then?' so the cop had to let him off. And of course he does a bit of band playing and that, but –' She hadn't known she was about to be serious, because usually she didn't show her serious side: it embarrassed her.

'Another drink?'

'Mm,' she grinned. Yes, she did like him. It was weird this, the way that liking would come surging over you in waves like happiness did. 'I want my play to make people happy and sad at the same time – because

136

that's what life's like – I mean you can be laughing your head off and it's really kind of sad as well.'

He was really listening to her and that made her want to say more. 'I'm not sad about things – I used to be bored – but I'm not now. . . . I'll be leaving school in July and I can't wait.'

He nodded. 'And then?'

'Dunno.' She flung out her hands, he looked at their coffee-cream palms and at her long fingers. He couldn't get over how complete she was. Upstairs he'd been of a mind to seduce her, because of the big cushiony lushness of her breasts and belly and the way her buttocks humped like melons. But then again, something about the expression in her eyes had stopped him: she wouldn't be joking, he'd sensed, and that could be dangerous. You might never know where it would end – then again, he wished he had. The trouble about growing old was that you saw situations from many angles: if I did X, Y would result, and so in the end you did nothing; and another part of him, the snake (he referred to it invariably as the 'snake'), said, 'You'd really do that old cow one if you made it with her daughter. . .'

'Do you want to come with me to see a preview of an auction out in the country next Wednesday evening?' he asked her out of the blue.

Her eyes shot up and she grinned.

'Yeah, why not?'

She left soon after that, comforted by the idea of another meeting with him. As she looked at him standing in the doorway, she was momentarily tormented by the idea that she might never see him again. Her mother used to call it Cordelia's 'I-want-it-now' mood. And most of the time it was still like that. She yearned to possess whatever it was that second –

137

and now, she thought he might die before she had chance to see him again, and that would be terrible. The touch of his finger nails gently edging along her cheek threw her into confusion. Marvellous, yummy, devastating! The unknown lay before her. . . . The trouble was you might be so scared you couldn't enjoy it: nuclear bombs threatening at any second, everything sinking into doom and gloom but nevertheless this continuing sense of the splendour of what was happening and would still come about.

She wondered as she cycled home whether he, despite his great age, could still feel the same thrill – thrill about what? She didn't know how to put it into words – this was all so new, it was like the excitement of groping to express something on paper, or like the moment when the curtain went up at the theatre and you knew that the magic was about to take over.

The plane trees and the limes swayed in a bright green arc above her. The limes were flowering and their blossom was yellow and powdery and dripped a sweet sticky substance onto pavements – it was warmish. She thought about the impending court appearance and she didn't care – it would after all be an adventure. This day, this minute, this ecstasy of being young and magnetised by the nasty, Brocklesby, kept her floating as on a huge air-cushion right up to her own door.

Chapter 15

The work-room rustled and banged with turbulence. Ted Smales had stopped wearing his special allure cream taken from the glands of some hapless monkey, which was supposed to send females into passionate transports but in fact only caused his tabby cat, Chole, to swarm up his crimplene trousers pulling threads. This lack of effort to attract on Ted's part meant that he had withdrawn into one of his cyclical depressions.

Sue noticed this at once because the musty smell was absent. 'She says that's absolutely it!' Ted rumbled on that Tuesday afternoon when they were sitting side by side at the working-surface.

'Oh yes. . .' Sue knew all this already as Tracy had told her so over tea in the students union. As the pinball machines had crashed and tinkled and pop music had bellowed hoarsely, Tracy's pekinese face had turned to her. 'Oh, Christ, I mean to say, Sue, you can't carry on like that. . . . I'd figured if I got preggers at the beginning of term I could have the baby in the summer – and now look at this –'

Tracy was furious, her eyes had bulged with malevolence, and she had sunk lower into her chins. Sue watching her had been intrigued but also shocked.

Tracy's main need was to control – here she had failed to bend nature to her will.

Ted handed her a bag of sunflower seeds. 'Good for you,' he muttered, 'might be a vegetarian soon – I keep saying next week. . . . I get this steak and I think, yes, think about battery farming and all those antibiotics they inject into cattle – unethical – and then –' he sighed as he stared at the black and white striped seeds.

Above, facing them, was the poster about poly-unsaturated fats, flanked by 'Desiderata'. Sue chomped her seeds and looked at the patterns in the loo-type glass.

It being Tuesday she and Ted invariably found themselves side by side in the work-room as they were on 'College Duties'. Their ruminations were inter-rupted by the report of the work-room door as it thudded open. Glynn Braithwaite flung in. He was about five-foot eight and weighed fifteen and a half stones. His passionate face glared at them. Glynn Braithwaite was the departmental Communist, the fervent believer in nuclear disarmament, and the liberator of women, blacks and the physically and mentally handicapped.

' "Something is rotten in the state of Denmark" ', Sue murmured.

'What?'

'Nothing –'

'What's up, mate?' Ted turned his attention momentarily to Glynn.

'Up – up? Seen Wendy?'

Wendy was his wife and had recently joined the staff.

'No.'

With that Glynn was gone. A draught of air swept papers from the tables and made the notices judder. There were so many bearing the words IMPORTANT, underlined and boxed in red, that no one bothered to read them or even saw them anymore for that matter.

Ted raised his eye-brows. 'What's bitten him?'

'He'll be having a row with Wendy. She told me he never does a thing at home – she's expected to see to the kids, do absolutely everything, whilst he lounges about – fat slob! She keeps freaking out with migraine and yet he only has to smile in her direction and she'll get on doing the housework again.'

Ted took a massive handful of seeds and jammed them into his mouth. He was so far removed from any shared domestic situation, that just the mention of other people's arrangements tended to make him thoroughly uneasy.

Sue looked at the pile of marking in front of her and poked her nails with the top of a red biro.

Last night's dream emerged as distinctly as any day-time happening. She saw Graham, the art student, her first love. He had been very beautiful that young man, she remembered, blond haired and finely proportioned. She had loved to watch him stretching or simply walking about; he had been agile, aware of his body and integrated with it in a way she hadn't been. She'd thought herself too tall for a woman and had walked hunched, considering herself to be totally outside the limits of what would have been deemed conventional good-looks.

Away from home for the first time as an under-graduate, she had been living alone in a flat. Graham had come there on warm summer afternoons. They had drunk Coke, squatting on a mattress on the floor, and had talked about his course or hers and his efforts to be a successor to Picasso. How desperately she had wanted him to make love to her. She had chosen him to be her first lover – she had been a virgin and had

141

wanted to rid herself of the limitations of that state. But he had refused – completely and utterly refused. She could kiss him, touch him all she liked but he would remain aloof – a Rodin man, sculptured in white marble. She had wanted him extravagantly and could not understand his refusal.

In desperation she had turned to another student. Lee Wild. He had been pleasant enough, but she hadn't desired him. The whole affair – it had only lasted a couple of encounters in his flat – had been without sparkle, lemonade with the fizz gone. Then she had bumped into her Rodin man and taken up the relationship as before, knowing with certainty that anything their bodies might have done together would have been right.

Now in the dream she had seen the two men, Graham and Lee, as middle-aged men: Lee was bald and long wispy hair clung to the outer edges of his pate, and Graham's blond hair had been dyed yolk yellow. They were embracing as two lovers and she, who had been, prior to Lee's entry into the room, kissing Graham, found herself abandoned. Feelings of anger and distress had caused tears to fill her eyes – she was a fool, a fool but mustn't let them see it. At that point the shrilling of the alarm clock had woken her.

These dreams returned at odd times so that her waking life was peopled with them. She felt that she had really seen Graham and Lee twenty years on. What did happen to beautiful young men?

'Sue?' Ted's voice droned plaintively.

'Mm?'

'I'm just working out this terrific scheme for second-year plumbers General Studies –'

'Oh good!' She realised she would certainly have to listen to Ted creaking into some act of sublimation. It

142

was curious how he had been drawn into Tracy's plan, being at first passive and indifferent and then becoming involved, but all on a muddled, negative level.

Halfway through the description of his scheme, Sue felt a hand on her thigh and his little bottle-glass lenses were turned to her, the tadpoles swimming behind the glass focused on her. 'Don't forget, gal – I'm always at your service!'

'Yes, Ted, I know you are!' Sue gave him a friendly pat as she would a dog or a horse. She did like him. He wasn't, thank God, a saviour of mankind like Glynn Braithwaite, or a beautiful person like golden-haired Graham – but he had no bleak side. His passion, if there was any, scrunched its way through pounds of sunflower seeds.

When she arrived home from work that afternoon, she found her parents waiting for her – she was expecting them.

'It's lovely here!' Mary Edwards said, glancing about.

'So you like it then!' Sue recalled how her mother had once been over-critical of her establishment. Her father was oddly shrunken and nervous, quite different from the father of her youth. Even the smallest jobs exhausted him. He sat in an armchair glancing through a newspaper, whilst Sue and her mother wandered out into the garden.

'He's so autocratic,' Mary was saying, 'since his coronary. You know, with him being at home all the time, he's nothing else to do but watch the dust settling – and I –' Mary stopped at the top of the garden path and looked at the yellow tea-roses and the honeysuckle climbing over the rustic arch. It was June and summer burgeoning.

Sue listened. The sight of her father's infirmity had

143

hurt her – but here was something else. She waited . . .
oddly enough she felt herself to be much more aware of
the nuances underlying people's words, in a way she had
never been before.

Mary was again struck by the starkness of her
daughter's outline as she had been during that weekend
visit when John had been lying in the Intensive Care
Unit. She envied her her self-sufficiency and indepen-
dence. If only she could herself do something exciting –
but would she dare?

'I like to –' she broke off, 'you're really making this
garden wonderful – what a parsley patch and the
potatoes and rhubarb – it's terrific!' Sue had always been
so untidy as a girl – the mess in her room: she never could
forget that litter of things, the confusion. She had
expected it somehow to engulf her daughter's life. But
now she saw it hadn't. Perhaps all that polishing and
fettling and vacuuming was a waste of time! Could it be?

'I might live another twenty years,' Mary said, as she
stared away over the compost heap to the high privet
hedge and the terrace beyond the disused railway track.
Blackbirds sang and sequences of notes echoed and
re-echoed down the long secret backs.

'Yes?' Sue waited.

'I – they seem to think that after a certain age women
cease to exist. Sue – I say to myself, what have I done?'

Sue was shocked by this. It was as though that
fortress, which she had always taken for granted, was
crumbling.

'You've brought up a family,' she managed.

'But I don't want to moulder now.'

They heard the frail and imperious voice calling from
indoors and turned back. Sue put her arm round her
mother's waist.

144

Chapter 16

Cordelia sat beside Brocklesby in his white Jag. It hovered over the road like a great pale moth in the early evening. The weather was perfect. Heat had lain over the town all day and been trapped between the brick terraces. Moon-pennies and tissue-paper-thin scarlet poppies crowded fields of high sappy grass. Cordelia gazed about her in excitement.

'This is ace!' she breathed.

'Good – what's been happening then?'

'I've nearly finished it –'

'Oh yes – what happens?'

'Lynne goes off to this peace camp. Mandy joins a band as a singer and Debbie takes an overdose.'

'Overdose – what for?'

'Cause she's fed up with living.'

Brocklesby was obviously rather shocked.

'But she's a bit young for that.'

'Quite a few people of that age kill themselves. Rachel Wittington in our class did last year.'

'Why?'

'She was fed up, I think.'

Cordelia was disturbed by his fingers on the wheel and the curve of his greyish cheek. She giggled. Oh but it was exciting, it was like munching through packets of chocolate digestive biscuits . . .

The house was about fifteen miles out in the country, a red-brick Georgian residence, set amid a group of elms. All the contents were to be sold by auction the following day.

'God, the haunted house!' Cordelia said enthusiastically. Brocklesby grunted and said nothing.

Together they approached the frontage. Cordelia's bare legs were tickled by high coarse grass. The day's heat was cooling now but the air was deliciously warm, it rippled over them like a tropical sea. Cordelia thought of surf breaking on white beaches and long-stemmed palms -- her father's country – though it probably wasn't like that at all.

They passed from room to room consulting the sale catalogues and turning things over. There were one or two good pieces of Victorian and a blue and green jardiniere which Cordelia admired.

Here and there Brocklesby put a cross and a note. He examined everything in an apparently off-hand way but in reality with great thoroughness.

'Okay, shall we go?' Brocklesby said at last.

Cordelia nodded.

'Like a drink before we finish?' She grinned enthusiastically.

They went into a country pub called The Green Dragon. Cordelia was intrigued by the inn sign with its energetic-looking dragon spuming forth red and yellow tongues of flame.

Inside it was cool and superior and the light seemed tarnished by comparison with the sunlight outside. Cordelia drank sherry and Brocklesby had his usual yellow drink. He was half turned towards her, studying her face and she felt a strong desire to giggle with delight. She put a hand up to her throat and felt its warmth and softness, her heart was beating strongly. From her throat to the soles of her feet, she felt conscious of her body – alive and fluid and excited. For minutes together they didn't say anything and then he put out his hand and let it rest on her thigh. His fingers slithered about on top of the silky material. It felt as though a sheet of flame were engulfing her legs: so this was what it was about – she had suspected as much.

Quite as abruptly he withdrew his hand and she felt bereft. Why wouldn't he go on – she could have killed him for not pursuing her.

In the strange twilight which had that honey gloss of old Dutch Masters, they drove back with the car windows wound down. She was being disloyal, stupid – everything together and she didn't care. She wondered what her unknown father would have thought – he could have disapproved of the age-gap no doubt.

'Where'll I drop you?' he asked, after they had been silent for a long time.

'Your house.'

This was his chance – if he wanted to seduce her, then she intended that he should have the opportunity.

'Coming in?'

'For a minute p'raps –'

In the mottled hall, where ruby and brown and gold shifted like dreams, they kissed for the first time. Her mouth filled with saliva. He was very gentle, but insistent enough for her to feel his sinuous intentness. She became paralysed. He took her hand and led her up the dark staircase. Coolness washed over them.

Cordelia was enchanted.

His bedroom was stark and white. She stood facing him and he removed the paste brooch at her cleavage. Slowly, taking his time, he undid the buttons on her

147

bodice. She turned and saw a huge ivory Buddha smiling at her. All of him seemed to be glowing, one curve passed into another. His belly was a magnificent white pumpkin. The lobes of his ears were pear blossom petals. Oh, she moaned, falling back against the white softness of the bed. All of her seemed to be gushing liquid. He removed his own clothes, at the same leisurely, flowing pace and in silence.

She lay back, waiting for him, watching him through half-closed eyes. His body was firmish but moving into slight corpulence over the belly – he was some Buddha sitting astride her. His thighs nipped hers together. With his finger-tips he was caressing the frills of flesh between her legs. She sighed again and a hot thrill of excitement tightened down her thighs. He sucked her brown pointed nipples and placed kisses between her breasts.

'Please, please,' she sighed.

After that it took a while and it burned and hurt. She saw the sweat on his face.

'You should have told me,' he said afterwards when they were lying side by side. 'You should have said, and I wouldn't have –'

She giggled against his shoulder. She had the impression that this might be something she would like very very much – quite adore in fact.

'Look, time's going on – would you like some peppermint tea?'

She'd never drunk such a thing in her life. Still nude she lay on his bed, gazing dreamily at the Buddha until he returned with a tray and shell-like china cups of a pale pink and green pattern. The tea was very thin and refreshing and smelt of peppermint and he brought chocolate biscuits in a small dish. The chocolate was dark and bitter. Oh the bliss of it, fragrant tea and 'chockie' biscuits and her own monster . . .

His lips brushed her shoulder. He had put on a navy-blue silk dressing-gown.

'Your mother'll be wondering what happened?'

'Yes –' Cordelia giggling, scoffing her fifth biscuit. She didn't feel like leaving a bit.

'Come on, don't want any trouble.'

At that she seemed to waken up as though from a dream. Still in the same half-waking half-asleep state, she dressed, drank two more cups of peppermint tea and fastened her brooch. Would they ever meet again? He smiled at her, differently from the way he had before – gentler now. He squeezed her fingers, lifted her hand to his lips and kissed it. The eloquence of that gesture left her quite overcome: at the same time she was thinking, 'If I ever write a love scene, I must be sure to remember that – just that, no words, just the hand –'

She wanted to tell him it was about the most marvellous thing she had ever experienced in her life, but she didn't because he would no doubt have known many such times. Determined not to refer to any future meeting unless he did, she ran down the long staircase. She was suddenly becoming afraid because, after all, it was late and her mother would be uneasy – there had been a number of murders and rapes in the town very recently; one woman had been murdered in broad daylight. Guilt left her speechless.

He followed her to the door. The brown gloom of the hall sprinkled with orange light from the lamp made his face appear rather white.

'Well?' he said, turning her to face him at the door. 'It's very late for you to be cycling home like this –'

'It doesn't matter. I'd knock anybody for six who tried to set about me –'

He smiled. 'Will you come again next week?'

'I might if you twist my arm –' She gave him a grin of release. Embarrassed and awkward she placed a clumsy kiss on his mouth.

'I'm twisting it!'

'Wednesday –'

'Agreed – eight?'

All the way home with the orange sodium lamps illuminating the alley of sycamores and limes, she returned over that amazing evening. She resented its abrupt interruption. Why had she got to leave, just when she would have wanted to linger on, losing herself in strange voluptuous mazes? She couldn't think past the moment. It came to her that she would never forget that evening and in future years its beautiful outline would emerge more clearly. At the point of its happening its strength and unfamiliarity did in a sense blur it – she was both caught in its vortex and standing back.

Chapter 17

The court-case was dismissed. In the evening there was a heavy thunderstorm. They were grouped about Linda's kitchen, waiting for the celebration dinner which was cooking in a casserole in the oven – one of Linda's chicken and wine concoctions, liberally spiced with garlic and thyme.

Robin and Tom were still recounting bits about the court-room scene. 'Christ, there were all these tattooed kids and the Dads with their flat caps on, looking dead gloomy and quite a few girls – some of 'em had about ten studs in each ear. I heard this girl say to this kid, 'I'll send you a v.o. . . . .' It was packed – and then there were little legal wallahs nipping up and down, real smart in their sharp suits and with the old brief-cases –'

'It was dreadful,' Robin murmured. 'You've never seen anything like it. It struck me that it was really all about games and rules: one class has set out the rules for the game and the other won't accept them – or even that there's a game. That's what crime's about. Criminologists might as well cease writing their tomes –' Robin gave one of his little enigmatic smiles and blinked, Linda thought he really ought to see an optician. 'I get the feeling that it's all been happening in

151

exactly the same way for hundreds of years – you just have to sit back and let yourself be processed, rather like sinking into a bath chair in a twilit home.'

'Christ, Robin, you do go on!' Tom exclaimed. 'Listen, there's work to be done! I'm going to get it – on an evening like this nobody'll be around, they won't exercise their dogs in the middle of a thunder storm. They'll just leave it – I'll get it, you watch!'

Robin looked startled, 'But –'

'No, I'm going to do this if it's the last thing I ever do –'

Linda was sitting smoking and drinking white wine and Sue was sprawling opposite her. It had been a very warm day.

'. . . so you see,' Linda was saying, 'the old Oxford trip fetched us a bomb in. If I could do a couple of those a month, I'd be making something. It'll mean though that I'll have to do considerably more buying in – and that means more auctions – which I love –' Linda's eyes were sparkling. It had been an extraordinarily interesting trip and Robin had proved very useful in that he had co-driven, helped in the lugging about of the goods and had been a chameleon-like companion. Yes, she decided, looking across at his hennaed tulip head, she did like him. He had a whole host of lavatory anecdotes which amused her – being a loo-attendant seemed rather like being a ferry-man: it was symbolic, people were going on a journey. . . . Linda grinned, sneezed and swallowed a gulp of wine which made her choke.

'Steady on –' Sue leaned across to slap her on the back. 'What's up?'

'Nothing, I was just thinking –'

'Where's Cordelia?'

'Out somewhere – it's getting late, isn't it? She's

becoming very vague about where she goes – and she's got a habit of turning up about midnight –' Linda's face grew lumpy with concern. 'I don't like it –'

'Well, as long as . . .' Sue usually played things down and went on about individual liberty, remembering her own struggles with her father over coming-in times. She had been sharply guarded and assiduously chaperoned as a teenager.

'No,' Linda sighed, 'I'll have to have it out with her – damn it! I ought to know what's happening, oughtn't I?'

'See you later,' Tom announced.

'Hey?' Linda's eyes shot up, 'what's on?'

'It's just a slight diversion. Back later –'

'What do you mean?'

'Tata –'

Tom and Robin made off. The women heard the front door thud to.

'Now what's that about?'

'The lamp-post!' Sue said because she had been following the dialogue.

'Oh God, what next – just what next. No sooner are we out of one jam than we're catapulting towards another. I'm sick –' Linda flung out an arm wildly and snatched her wine glass. 'And Cordelia – what the hell has got into her?'

The casserole continued to bubble gently in the oven.

'You know how I am, I generally sit back and I say everybody has to do his or her own thing – don't I?' Linda looked across at her friend, and Sue nodded. 'There's no point in trying to stop somebody – I realise you can't make somebody else happy. People have to work out their own pattern. Only when it comes to your own kids, it's hard –'

153

Sue yawned and nodded again. 'True. . . . Oh, lady, I'm dying for a holiday. Do you know, I'm knackered: I wake up in the morning and I feel exhausted. Oh Christ – what classes, there I am flogging myself to death and I think, what's it for, why am I killing myself when they don't care –' Sue took a long swallow of wine.

It was always like this in the summer term – lethargy, irritation, bursts of anguish and *Weltschmerz*. They all began to question the daily plod. It went roughly: what am I doing here, why am I sitting in this barn-like hall invigilating, or in this stuffy work-room marking exam scripts? Just beyond the glass tooth or the crumbling hall nirvana must surely lie.

'I wonder what the three sisters would have done had they reached Moscow?' Sue speculated, taking another long slug of wine.

'Started longing for Paris,' Linda remarked drily. 'Now I've told you, I've seen this superlative shop – right in the centre – it'ud just be the thing for me.'

'Well and what's the snag?'

'The property belongs to bloody B., big bloody B.'

Just then they heard the front door banging. 'Cordelia!' Linda called. 'Cordelia!' She wanted to make sure that the girl didn't escape upstairs.

Cordelia appeared in the doorway. She was drenched and her dress was sticking to her like a second skin.

'Where've you been?' Linda asked and her eyes gleamed savagely.

'Out.'

'Out won't do, I want to know where –'

'To see Debbie –'

There was something about Cordelia and Linda became instantly aware of it in that moment as she looked at her daughter's face which was slippery with

154

water – a certain new energy. It seemed to beam out of her. This aura suggested an alien world – where had she been? Not to Debbie's mother's council house – that brick box like so many others squatting amongst the metal clothes poles and identical strips of garden. No, Linda knew enough about life to suspect something different. She fought the surfacing of her own early conventional life – the housewife-of-the-year period.

'I'll go and get dry,' Cordelia said and disappeared upstairs. They heard the creaking of the banisters and the staircase as she bounded up.

'That kid's up to no good,' Linda remarked darkly.

'You're too anxious. I'm surprised at you, Linda, you're so together and then suddenly you freak because old Cordelia's been late in a few times – she can handle it. You're becoming one of those fathers who watch their daughter's virginity like guard-dogs: they almost make on think they'd like to have a go themselves. That's how I always used to feel about Dad – if I ever thought about it. All good Freudian stuff.'

They listened to the rain drumming on the bay for a while.

'Okay,' Linda said, 'I suppose you're right, only –'

'Come on! Tell me about the shop.'

Just then Cordelia re-emerged in her jeans and T-shirt.

'So the property belongs to that old buzzard, he'll never part with it to me – I wouldn't want it – and I'd set my heart on it, you know that. I really wanted it – no joke, I really did –' Linda sighed. 'I could see my gear set out, water-coolers, everything –'

Cordelia had sat down on the floor and was playing nervously with the bottom of her T-shirt, winding it round her fingers. Sue saw her own mother's hands pleating something, pushing her nervousness into the

155

folds of material – what was the matter with Cordelia? In the space of a few months she had changed. Or was she imagining it? Strange how alterations in contour were often more difficult to detect in familiar landscapes than in unknown ones.

Listening to her mother, Cordelia was filled with dread and also anger and exasperation: why couldn't she see that Brocklesby wasn't really a baddy? She'd made up her mind about him long ago and she wasn't ever going to re-think it. It was as though in a sense she had become blind. How odd that was! She wondered if she herself was so closed about other people.

Whilst she was waiting for the moment of tension to pass, she was also thinking of that evening of a few hours ago: how she had walked up to him in the hall, literally trembling, and he had slid his hands down her throat, her breasts, her belly – and in his white room where the Buddha smiled welcome, they had taken it very easy, revisiting the curve of a shoulder, a thigh, those secret places. Sex contained the world: it was wild, delirious, thrusting, enclosing, free. She thought of him all the time, of his own unknown body, of his strangeness. He was a hundred other people whom she would never know except in flashes now and then – and there were areas of deadness in him when he seemed to switch off and she would feel how his attention had left her and she would want it restored instantly. If only she had been older – ten, fifteen years, twenty – and then that gulf would not have yawned so darkly: it represented almost a life-time – oh but she was lonely! She couldn't wait to be back there. They had eaten peaches from a white china bowl and the juice had run down her chin and he had licked it up whilst lying with his arm under her neck. His hand had traced patterns over her breasts and just before the storm they had smelt the scent of limes drifting in through the open window – sweetness, fragrance that lulled you. She had covered him with sticky juice and licked him, watching the strange mollusc-like object lengthening and strengthening until it jerked and would thrust.

'Sue,' she chanced, 'I've er – done a play –'

'A play!'

Both the older women looked at her in surprise.

'Yes, I want to get somebody to perform it –'

'A play!' Linda felt she must re-appraise the situation yet again. So that girl had written a play, this kid who was according to her teachers supposed to be useless at school and could hope for very little in the choice of employment, she had managed to. . .

'Can I have a look then?'

'Okay, I'll get it – but don't laugh at me, will you?'

They listened to the familiar thunder of Cordelia's feet on the stairs.

'I wouldn't have believed it –' Linda said.

'Why not? You're surprising me tonight, old girl.' Sue stretched her toes and kicked off her 1940s sandals.

'Here, give me a roll-up for Christ's sake!' Linda muttered, grining slyly, 'that's if you haven't given up!'

'Enough digs. All right – here, I'll make it myself –'

'Do you suppose the police have captured those two again?' Linda asked suddenly.

'No, I expect they're deciding to give it up as a bad job – they'll never pull it up.'

'It's become more than a lamp-post.'

'I know – it's like Everest, or rather the climbing thereof. Linda,' Sue said, 'have you got an Everest?'

She thought for some time. 'Yes – that shop. I want it, I've wanted it – I know I can make it pay because quite simply I have a way with good gear.'

'Well,' Cordelia said, bursting into the room with some of her former abandonment, 'this is it!' She held out a couple of exercise books to Sue. She was feeling tremulous about her play because perhaps she had been foolish in imagining that it could amount to anything at all. It had belonged to her until that second and only Brocklesby knew of its existence. Even as she was handing it to Sue, part of her wanted to take it back – but she needed to know Sue's response. She was at pains to hide her feelings – nobody must know how seriously she felt about it.

'Thank you. I'll read it tonight before I go to bed, Cordelia, then perhaps we can have a natter about it –'

Cordelia went out to the back door. Suddenly the room seemed stiflingly hot. She opened it and stood on the doorstep. The rain had stopped and the chimney pots placed here and there amid the grass and shrubs stood out distinctly like the doric columns of some pagan temple. A moon was beginning to emerge from the banks of cloud and the evening was milky and warm. Gnats danced in formation. From the bottom of the ten-foot came a hooting.

'They're back!'

Cordelia raced off in the twilight and encountered her brother and Robin who were lovingly examining the huge rusting shaft of the aged lamp-post. On the arm the magic words, 'Victoria Dock' were inscribed.

'Now what about that?' Tom asked triumphantly. Robin was running his fingers down the bevelled sides. 'It's really very beautiful!' he muttered softly.

'How the devil did you get it up?' Cordelia wanted to know.

'Same as before – just dragged – and finally up it came!'

'Brilliant!'

Sue and Linda walked slowly down the path. '. . . and your Everest?' Linda was asking.

'I'm wondering whether I've got one anymore. Now, isn't that strange? If you'd asked me a month ago, I'd have said –'

'The lamp-post!' Linda strode round the pick-up, examining its elegant proportions. 'This is quite perfect! I can just see it standing in front of the shop –'

'That's what we got it for.'

'We'll have to paint it a lovely chocolate colour.'

'Lamp-posts ought to be black,' Sue chipped in.

'No, it's got to be chocolate –' Linda stood firm. 'I'll sand it down with my orbital sander and undercoat it and then paint it – a true work of reclamation!' She gave her witch's neighing gurgle, which finished in a smoker's cough.

'Are we getting a drink and nosh on it then?' Tom asked.

'Oh yes, the celebration. Of course there must be a celebration. The grub's in the oven –'

They spread themselves comfortably in the kitchen and another bottle of wine was uncorked and Linda brought out the big earthernware casserole. They sat at the farm-house table tearing at the garlic bread and smiling. Linda was still preoccupied with how she might get the shop, and had momentarily forgotten her disquiet about Cordelia – and she? She was elated but disturbed: Sue would soon be turning the pages of the exercise books, reading her secret imaginings – she felt she was on the verge of something. Sue was looking around at the faces of them all in the room and grinning. Tom was some brown Hamlet – and Robin? He had a gentleness about him which she liked. He was delicately stripping off pieces of crusty bread and licking his fingers – and there was Linda – she saw them

159

all in a sudden still. And outside a war was raging. Every news broadcast spoke about the war in the Falklands. Cars bore stickers 'I'm British, so are the Falklands'. She took a deep draught of white wine, on the brink of chaos life felt so good. She was reluctant to go next door to her own home, but she remembered her promise to read Cordelia's play – and of course tomorrow was work. The play had roused her curiosity.

It was three thirty in the morning when Sue left, and the sky was light grey and as she stood a moment looking down the still road, she wondered whatever was going to happen to them. Mostly she was too busy to think about it – but that night, what with the wine and celebration, she felt unusually pensive.

Chapter 18

'The play is very, very good,' Sue told Cordelia. 'I couldn't put it down. I finished it when it was light, I had to –'

Cordelia felt a sudden flood of embarrassment making her cheeks hot. She was momentarily speechless and stared down at her hands.

'We must try to get it performed.'

'Oh . . .' Cordelia still seemed unable to speak.

'With this present interest in women's drama, we could try to interest a women's group in it – perhaps a local one? Shall I make some enquiries?'

'Great. Yeah, sure –' Cordelia twiddled about on one foot and fiddled with the buttons on her shirt. She was oddly subdued.

'We've really got to see that it's performed, it's about important things. Leave it with me then, I'll see what I can find out.'

Cordelia walked into town. She was in a curious frame of mind. She couldn't really believe that the play was good. Sue's words has shocked her: she must be joking, or being enthusiastic because she wanted to encourage her. As well as that she felt moody and disturbed as though she could cry at the least provocation, which was totally unlike her. She prided herself on being tough and not giving in to things. She felt she wanted to talk to bad B. and she wasn't to see him until Friday at the earliest – they met by appointment within a formal framework.

In the city centre she met a group of girls from school who were likewise just wandering. People tended to saunter about in droves because most couldn't think of anything to do – which was not so in Cordelia's case – although they were supposed to be revising. The clever ones of course would be swotting at home for their 'O' Levels – they still thought they had some prospects.

Cordelia exchanged a few desultory words with the others and then drifted away on her own. She had basically nothing to tell them. They were discussing the new mini skirts they wanted to buy, or some boy they had met. She was moving into an altogether more exotic region.

In the centre of the town near the Whaling Museum and Art Gallery there was a public garden. It had been laid out on the site of an old dock. Neat flowerbeds, small conifers, a rose arbour and two ponds formed a symmetrical pattern. Finding that she was feeling very odd indeed, Cordelia sauntered into the garden and sat down on one of the wooden benches. She could see the grey stone frontage of the museum and it reminded her of school trips and the pathetic keening sound of a whale which met you as you entered one of the lower rooms. She had been chilled by its unearthly note. Some of the kids had laughed, others had been unsure. Menacing had been the gigantic skeleton of the whale which occupied the entire length of the building.

She leaned back against the bench. Strong sunlight caused the dwarf pines to give off a fragrance redolent of mysterious Eastern musks. She thought of the

162

Buddha's rounded white cheeks . . . 'What on earth will become of me?' she wondered. Her head ached and she felt sick and giddy. The brilliance of the sunlight oppressed her. Unemployed men were sitting on park benches staring indifferently at the day. Presently they got up and left. She was alone. Moor hens zigzagged on the ponds amongst the bulrushes and reeds, the lily pads stirred on their long jade stalks. She imagined them twining and twisting, lying in wait for any swimmer – if you were to jump in there, they would cling about you, dragging you down. Yes, if you were simply to walk off the edge and drop in . . .

Lines from the play kept coming back to her and muddling in her head so that her feeling of sickness increased. Everything seemed to be distorted as in one of the mirrors at the fair. She remembered walking over a path which rocked from side to side and at the same time seeing herself in a distorting mirror. Her cheeks had ballooned out – she was squashed and dwarf-like, then suddenly thin and elongated, a Jack Sprat.

Life had been simple before. Well, perhaps not exactly straightforward but not like this. There were two possibilities – run away to London, or jump in the pond or off the pier. An overdose? She would never see him again – not ever, ever. Why did there have to be such elaborate rules for living?

A gang of denim-clad youths, one or two with their heads shaved and their arms covered with blue tracery, were marching up the flagged paths by the rose-arches. Their boots rang out aggressively as they approached. People got out of their way. Those lying in the grass eyed them warily. Cordelia registered the faint stirrings of apprehension in her stomach. She was afraid but there was nothing she could do – they were too close

163

for that. She kept her gaze fixed on the ground. The boots came on. The were cursing in the loud-crude tone which she had so often heard. It was nothing new to her.

'Coon!' a voice jeered. She still refused to look up. 'Coon – wog – wogs out! Niggers out! What you doin' in this country? Get back where you belong!'

Her heart was banging so hard she felt faint. She looked up then, directly into their challenging faces. It was the yowl of the back-streets and poverty, that she was hearing. Rage and terror constricted her guts.

'I was born here,' she said very cool, swallowing her fear.

'You should get back where you belong, you nigger cunt!'

'If I'd got a knife,' she thought, 'I'd stab each of you.' Her anger was greater than her fear. She hadn't known she could feel such rage.

'Fuck off!' she snarled. If it came to it, she would fight, They'd not finish her without a struggle.

'Go fuck yourself!' a bald youth with a face like a scraped potato bellowed. He moved up to her with his fist raised. 'I'll smash your fuckin' teeth down your gob, you cunt!'

And then the two businessmen entered the garden with their executive cases flashing importantly. The group kept going, banging their feet as they went.

Cordelia sank back, limp with relief. Tears began to tumble down her cheeks. Her throat hurt with the effort of trying to repress them. In the end she didn't even try – she went on crying silently with the sun blazing down on her face.

There were, she decided, far worse things than an overdose or jumping off the pier. It was the first time in her life that she had ever been so physically afraid of

164

something. She felt very muddled up: here was horror, not long before she had experienced what she could only term 'bliss'. Was this feeling with Brocklesby what people called 'love' – it must surely be. The songs crooned about it, people in magazines talked about it. Characters in books asked one another, 'Do you love him?' Sue didn't believe in love – she was sure her mother didn't either. She hadn't thought about whether she did or not – but now it had come unasked – it and more . . . so much more than now she was overwhelmed by it.

Chapter 19

'Well,' Linda asked, 'what did you really think of it?'

'It's very, very good: she's got a feel for words – for dialogue. She's captured what people really say. I felt for those kids all the way. It's a mixture of the funny and the brash, and then pathos comes in. I was weeping myself by the end when the kid takes an overdose.'

'My goodness!'

'I've already had a word with this theatre group who're trying to promote "Women in Theatre" and I've given it to them to have a look at.'

'I wish she'd be a bit more communicative. She used to be so different – I suppose this is adolescence.'

Linda was sitting in a deckchair in Sue's garden. It was a balmy evening. The hot spell had continued and the sky above the backs was a hazy opal shot through with gold. Gnats fluttered above the pond and now and then the water twitched slightly as something stirred the still black surface. Children's voices reached them from another garden which they couldn't see.

Linda was in a strange mood. The previous evening she had been rooting through some old photographs in a chest of drawers in her bedroom, when she had come across a photograph of her mother. On the snap she

166

was leaning against a stone wall and smiling into the camera. She had an air of vivacity in her sparkling eyes and the dimples by her mouth – young and beautiful she was. It struck her then as never before, how much her mother had suffered. And Linda had realised how harshly she had judged her. She had always thought her mother unloving, cold, somehow locked up in herself. There she was in the photo, full of youthful optimism, certain that the future most hold fulfilment, joy: but it hadn't, the joy had been in that moment when the shutter flashed, and in no other. After marriage had come endless domestic chores, a husband at war, who had come home broken in body and spirit, only to die prematurely of a chest ailment and later there had been very little else in her mother's life except the struggle for survival.

It was the fashion, she saw, for children to attribute all their present ills to their parents' mismanagement of their early childhood – Freud had succeeded only too well.

But it was that phantom mother who had stirred her oddly and caused her to cry – she who couldn't remember having cried for years. Tears had poured down her cheeks as she lay on her wide bed and stared at the ceiling. There was no way of redressing that wrong, of saying to her, 'I didn't see you properly, Mum,' because she was dead now. She had finished up in an old people's home, as she couldn't cope with living alone and none of the children had been able, for one reason or another, to take her to live with them. One Christmas she had been found dead in bed of pneumonia. None of them had ever been able to breach that plate-glass screen which had separated them from her. She had spent her days reproving them and they had avoided her, smarting under her criticism and her irritable moods.

'What's up?' Sue asked, refilling Linda's wine glass.

'Oh just thinking of my mother – wishing I'd

167

understood her better –'

'You feel you didn't?'

'No, I never understood her –'

They were silent for a while. Sue made two roll-ups and handed one to Linda.

'Things are in a very peculiar state at the moment. We were talking in General Studies about what each one of us would do if we were prime minister. This sweet, naive seventeen-year-old said, 'The police should be armed.' And you know when I expressed surprise, they all joined in, 'Oh yes, our cops must be armed – we need law and order, they should bring back capital punishment.' The kids seem to see monsters lurking round every tree. . . . Hey, and have you noticed how many people are buying those elaborate burglar-alarm systems? There are two shops selling them on the way into town. I look in every morning –'

'General hysteria –' Linda inhaled deeply, 'all that crap about the crime-rate rising, they're trying to pin the causes on the unemployed and the blacks . . . old folks think they're going to be mugged if they set foot out of doors –'

Linda felt somehow restored by this conversation. It heaved her up out of the trough of the past – most of which she had forgotten anyway: the husbands had been and gone and were now almost as though she had never known them. They all belonged to different compartments.

'I think I'd better go back to my place,' she murmured at last, 'I've been trying to organize some gear for next week's trip.'

'Well, I suppose I'd better do some registers. I hate it, but never mind.'

With that Linda crossed to her own house. Nobody seemed to be in. It occurred to her that she hadn't seen

168

Robin all day. She wondered when he would turn up. Cordelia was missing again. Tom was playing with his group. She began sorting through some tiles.

Sue continued to sit in the garden smoking and watching the flickers on the pond. Blackbirds trilled, flirting in the sycamores and the high privet rustled. She was still dwelling on that day's teaching. Whole classes would be momentarily captured by what the TV, the newspapers or the radio had been currently running – these were special topics or obsessions: you thought crime, immigration, nuclear war – until it all subsided like the sea ebbing and flowing. You, in the middle, had to remain constant – or like a prisoner in solitary confinement fix on something to see you through, whether match-sticks with which to construct miniature towns or budgerigars which you cooed at and taught your favourite expressions.

Tracy Pittaway had paid an enraged visit to her doctor, demanding to know why she had not conceived. He had been unable to tell her anything she wanted to hear, after all she was 'knocking on a bit' and as one grew older, one's fertility declined.

Ted was too busy trying to mark exam papers and totalling his great piles of registers to spare much time for anything else – and of course their present pains were being ameliorated by the constant reports of colleges in other parts of the country where their colleagues had been summarily made redundant.

Education for leisure, the changing form of education, of society – of this and that. . . . Sue had to smile, as she re-lit her roll-up and emptied her wine glass. In this situation you could feel either a) glad that you had a job still, and/or b) pleasantly titillated by the impending possibility of redundancy. It could afford endless opportunity for speculation. Sue yawned and

169

stretched, feeling neither sad nor glad – simply tired after the day's labours and curious to see what that night's dreams would bring. Who would come wandering through the little French window into the sitting-room? Who? Would it be the negro – *'Ich bin guter Hoffnung!'*: the brown arms sweeping up the woman's body into a soft cuddle, the laughter, the lurching to and fro in merriment. . .

Cordelia's play was still with her too, its verve and audacity, good old Cordelia. But what was wrong with her? Was this the result of artistic creation?

She thought of making tea – no more wine for the present – and she lurched down under the rose-arch to look at the vegetable patch which she was proudly tending: the triumph of eating her own potatoes, carrots, lettuce and courgettes! She stooped to inspect the lettuces for slugs. Slugs were an abomination with their slime and the way they chewed holes in the lettuce leaves turning them to tatters. It was sheer impossibility for her to touch them with bare hands, so she made a point of approaching them with her rubber gloves if she meant business. Everything looked healthy enough. The courgettes were forming. They had wedge-like phallic ends, blunt and swelling, and they were a vivid mottled green. Bright yellow flowers with sharp pointed petals covered the sinuous hairy stalks of the mother plants.

The moon swam up clear over the backs. It hovered over the line of terraces beyond the railway track. From several houses away came the thump of a transistor and then TV laughter and dialogue – it all seemed over-precise and even in key, not like real voices. Sue reflected how life was like a series of stills, placed one beside the other. The memory stored these: tonight it was haunting night-time beauty, it left her

170

awe-struck. She could feel like that too about man-made objects like old embroidery, 1920s dresses – and about people, the comfort of her friends, and recently now, her parents.

She straightened up and sauntered towards the house. On the doorstep she turned once and paused to gaze at the luminosity of the sky. She would have liked to read for a while, but wouldn't let herself. It had to be work.

Cordelia was cycling up the road under the moon and she saw Sue's light and wanted to go in. It would be easier to tell Sue – tell her what?

She had been to see him, had wandered in his garden with him and had then told him. He had been very grave.

'I should have known. I'm to blame all right . . . you'd think, at my age. . .'

'I'm supposed to know all about it, well, I do – but I didn't want to. . . . It's all so sordid – sort of calculating and I. . .'

This time it had happened in the front room by the jade Buddha, a long, slow release – another sweet foolishness.

Should she go in and speak to Sue, ask her advice? School was another world: 'Now have you all done your project?' Project was a word for boredom, for a time-wasting exercise. All these things seemed to happen to you when you were alone. Sue and her mother seemed so strong and complete. They just went on as though the world were not falling apart – but was it?

She got off her bike, propped it up against Sue's wall, gave her usual three blasts on the door-bell and walked in.

Sue was in the kitchen just making tea, when Cordelia pushed the door open.

'Oh, hi, I was just thinking about you. Tea?'

171

'Please.'

They looked at each other and smiled. 'Well, what's been happening? Thinking about your next play?'

'Sue, er –'

'Mm?' Sue tried to be as casual as possible.

'Something's happened.'

'Oh yes?'

'I think I'm expecting.'

Sue felt how the skin on her face went cold with shock, but she didn't show any surprise.

'Hm, that is new – would it, er, be inappropriate to enquire about the father?'

'That's just it.'

There was an awful pause and Sue sipped her tea. She could feel the droplets of perspiration forcing their way up on her nose and forehead.

'It's Brocklesby.'

'My God!' Sue scrabbled in her handbag for her tobacco tin and cigarette papers. 'Yes – this is news!' As she dribbled the tobacco along the paper, her head buzzed with jagged fragments. What now?

Cordelia, brave, gutsy Cordelia was crying and Sue abandoned all attempts at lighting her roll-up and put her arm round the girl.

'Don't worry, things'll sort themselves out –'

'Mum'll go mad, absolutely insane.'

'Take it easy, just get things in perspective –' Even whilst she was talking calmly and evenly Sue was trembling inside: Linda was bound to be immensely angry: the Montagues and Capulets – oh, that wouldn't be anything compared with the depths of Linda's fury. What did you say in these cases? Cordelia seemed to be calming down. After the first flood of tears, she was resting her face against Sue's shoulder.

'What, er, were you thinking of doing?'

172

'I don't know – I told him tonight.'

'And what did he say?'

'He said he'd behaved like a teenager and he seemed very disgusted with himself – and then he said would I, would I marry him.'

'My God!' Sue's eyes opened wide in disbelief, she let go of Cordelia and picked up her discarded roll-up, lit it, inhaled and took a long swig of cooling tea. To think that a few minutes previously she had been pottering contentedly in her garden, gazing at the lettuces and admiring the bulbous loveliness of her striped courgettes! Then the immediate world of house and garden had seemed so tranquil, so contented – and now this!

'And what did you say to that?'

'Nothing – I mean I didn't know what to say. I thought I'd better think about it . . . Mum's going to go mad –'

Tea, the pacifier and comforter – Sue poured it from one of her cockerel tea-pots. It issued in a thin brown stream.

'Sue – you know Mum won't hear anything good about Brocklesby – not ever. You know he's not bad – people are just good or bad depending on how you look at them. I mean it's not fair to dismiss them out of hand, is it?'

'No –' Sue looked through the window at the bone-white moon in the milky sky and she was unaccountably moved. Cordelia was so straightforward in her reaction, and that idealism could very easily be destroyed. 'I take it you want to have the baby?'

'Oh yes – well, I mean, it's mine, isn't it?'

'You wouldn't want an adoption?'

'Couldn't – I'd always wonder what had happened to it. I'd be so curious I couldn't bear it –'

173

'You're quite sure you're pregnant?'

'Yes, I must be –'

'Why on earth didn't you – ?'

'Because I never intended to – you don't exactly go looking for things and if I'd been swallowing pills, then I would have had it in my mind – and well, you see, I did it only because it was him –'

Sue tried to take it all in. Linda would have to be told.

'Your Mum'll wonder where you are for one thing. Now, shall I come across with you?'

'Sue, I'm so frightened. You can't imagine how it is – you see, all the time I felt sort of guilty about seeing him – but I couldn't stop.'

'Come on, let's get it over. Do you want me to come with you – or would you rather – ?'

'I don't want to go home.' Cordelia was starting to cry again. Sue hugged her.

'Let's go in and tell her. Your Mum's been through a lot in her life and she isn't unreasonable –'

Nevertheless Sue had grave doubts.

They went to Linda's house and Sue paused on the doorstep and turned to look up at the moon and the North star which she had never seen so bright: it really was 'like a diamond in the sky', a great nugget of brilliance. She took a deep breath. Cordelia was following her.

'This is the worst moment of my life –' Cordelia muttered. It was marginally worse than the confrontation in the park.

Linda was packing tiles and pieces of crockery into tea-chests and she had spread lots of things out on the living-room floor.

'Oh good! Look, I thought this might go down well – did I show you?' she held up a piece of framed tapestry

174

for Sue's inspection. It depicted a blonde-haired maiden holding a pitcher and the embroidery had been worked in various shades of cream and honey.

'That's great.'

'There you are!' Linda caught sight of Cordelia. 'Look at the time. I've just about had enough of it. Every time I –'

'It's all right, she's been having a very serious talk with me, Linda.' Sue drew on the stub of her roll-up. 'Can you spare a minute?'

Linda's head came up. Her grey frizzed hair swung back behind her shoulders. She was some gudgeon, gasping for air. She had sensed that something disastrous had happened.

'What is it?' she said, 'what's up. Don't mess about – tell me!'

'Mum, er – I'm pregnant.'

'I see –' Linda groped for her tobacco pouch and began lining a cigarette paper. There was a silence. 'What are you proposing to do about it?'

'Have the baby and keep it –'

'Hm.' Linda sat down heavily in her big springless chair, her knees wide apart, one elbow propped up on her right knee. 'You don't know what you're in for, lass. Oh, Christ, let's have some tea –'

'Okay, I'll see to it.' Sue went off to fill the kettle and plug it in. She felt for both women. She'd never experienced Cordelia's rapture about a man – or had she? One forgot. Nevertheless it seemed fitting to her in a certain way that the baby should have been the result of such a union. On the other hand Linda could appreciate the day-to-day awfulness of the life which Cordelia might have to lead and the limitations on her future ambitions.

When Sue got back into the room with the tray and

175

the tea Linda still didn't know the whole truth – obviously she hadn't asked about the father or even thought of him.

'. . .the sheer grind. Look, I was pregnant at about your age – with my first family. I'm telling you, Cordelia, it's not joy and manna overflowing. It's being tied all the time and done in and finding you can't go out dancing or to the pub or anywhere just when you like: you've another person to take into account.'

Sue handed round the tea. Cordelia was sitting on the edge of her chair like some visitor who had just dropped in. Suddenly she looked very old: Sue saw her how she might be in fifty years – and then what would this evening be, something to reminisce about with her grandchildren. That was if there was a world, and there were human-beings on it. Ghosts.

'Mum, I don't want an abortion, and I don't want to give it away – it's mine.'

Sue was back with her dreams – the massive, swelling gourd, the fecundity of 'Genesis'. How mysterious was the whole process of conception and pregnancy! She was struck by Tracy's view of conception and that of Cordelia.

'Think very carefully about it. I've tried to bring you up to be a person, to do your own thing, to be –' Linda's voice faded.

'But Mum, that's what I'm doing.'

'No, you're going into bondage without realising it.'

There was silence whilst they sat round drinking tea. It had grown very late and Sue became aware of the stillness outside them in the street.

'Well, you don't have to decide this second about it, do you – how far on?'

'Uh, well – it's six weeks since my period should have come.'

It was then that it seemed to occur to Linda that she hadn't asked about the father.

'And – and whose is it?'

The silence was gruesome. They could hear the spooky call of an owl. Linda's gaze was fixed intently on her daughter. Sue felt breathless, the house seemed suddenly oppressive with its hulking sideboards and dressers and mahogany tables. It seemed to her that the Georgian bureau-cabinet with its triangular broken pediment would topple forward and crush them all.

'Well – er, it's Brocklesby!'

'This is the end,' Cordelia was thinking. She became quite calm after the revelation.

Linda sat back now and began rolling another cigarette. She didn't say anything and her face remained flat and blank. Sue wished she'd rage and get it over, anything but this peculiar withdrawal.

And then it came. She lit her roll-up, took a long drag and then said very coldly, 'You fucking, little idiot – you've let him use you. I thought you'd more about you. I really did. My daughter and you opened your legs for – that toad. The last person in the world. . . . Oh Christ, and I thought you'd not make all the old mistakes. Why did I – ?'

Again silence came over them. Sue wished herself anywhere but there. She was incapable of saying anything – she heard her own words earlier. 'Oh, Cordelia knows how to handle it.' Linda had evidently been right to worry – but even had she tried to intervene, she could have changed nothing, only driven Cordelia more surely towards Brocklesby.

'I shall go to see him, the bastard –'

'Mum, you've got it wrong.'

'Yes, I would have –'

'He's not what you think –'

177

'What a monster, old enough to be –'

'Linda,' Sue tried, 'don't you think Cordelia should go to bed now – it's very late.'

Linda shot Sue a glance, seeming to see her for the first time. 'Oh yes, I suppose so. Go to bed, out of my sight –'

Cordelia stumbled out of the room and they heard her heavy, defeated steps mounting to the bedroom.

'We'd better have a gin.' Linda rose and took the gin bottle out of the eighteenth-century bow-fronted corner cupboard. Sue stared, as she had so often done, at the chinoiserie decoration and the butterfly hinges, only this time she didn't see them.

'How could she do this to me? How could she?'

'I don't suppose she intended to do anything to you,' Sue said gently.

'What a swine – he stops at nothing. He's a notorious womaniser – a very dangerous man. As though we didn't recognise the pattern . . . this whole scene makes me sick, I know it too well. And she wants to keep it, his – oh Christ!'

'What on earth will you say to him?'

'Does it matter? The swine –'

Sue finished her gin. 'We ought to go to bed, you know, it's work tomorrow, and before we know what the dawn chorus will have started up. I don't know what to say – try not to take it too hard, old lass –'

'Wouldn't you?'

'I suppose I would.'

'There you are then. I wanted her to be a person in her own right, do you understand – can't you see – I wanted to help her miss out some of the dross, short-circuit it. No chance – she has to go in for the full mortification. I didn't fill her head full of this love nonsense. You're lucky you've had the sense to steer

178

clear of it all –'

'It was nothing intentional. Look, Linda, I'm going. Sleep on it – tomorrow you might feel differently.'

Sue knew as she entered her own house, locked up and went upstairs to bed, that this was very unlikely. Linda would probably feel even worse after a sleepless night.

Chapter 20

As Sue had already surmised, Linda didn't sleep much that night. She lay on her back staring up at the plum-coloured ceiling, trying to digest what had happened. Had Cordelia been made pregnant by anyone else, she would have been sad, – yes, certainly sad – but this. . . . The very thought of the Obscenity, Brocklesby, seducing Cordelia, made her fumble on the small pine table by the bed for her tobacco tin and cigarette papers. With unsteady fingers she made a roll-up and levered herself into a semi-reclining position with the pillows stuffed behind her back.

She thought of her past struggles – that period in her life when she had felt there must be a man around. She supposed she had been so dependent on men simply because she'd known no other pattern. Once her father had died, her mother had become quite withdrawn, seeming unable to cope or take any interest in life. Her marriages had been fairly disastrous seen from some angles – but she had learned a lot from them. Surviving the divorces though had been hard. A long period of should-I, shouldn't-I? had preceded them, in which she had vacillated wildly, and had experienced panicky feelings at the thought of being alone – there would be no man, no sex – but she had soon realised there would also be no irritating restrictions on her self-determination, nobody to grunt and grumble and complain.

To enjoy that new freedom had been another effort. The pleasure had come slowly – just little things like learning to prepare meals for one, if the children happened not to be at home, to decide how to spend public holidays. . .

She had forgotten it all because it had happened long ago in the past, but now it was returning to her. Cordelia would be setting out on that path. 'I've failed with her,' Linda told herself, 'failed miserably, absolutely – just ridiculously failed –'

As she smoked her roll-up to the end, staring vaguely about the room with its flowered wash bowls and water jugs and ornate mahogany dressing tables and chests, she remembered what Sue had kept saying, 'Linda, I'm surprised at you –' Why was she surprised? She knew it must be because she had descended from her composure: just when she had been feeling fairly complacent, this had happened.

Ought she to have given Cordelia a pep-talk about contraceptives? But Cordelia knew – you couldn't force your daughter to go on the pill? You had to leave people a measure of privacy – she was no longer a child after all. But Brocklesby – why him? She had thought herself unshockable: she evidently wasn't. Years of looking at the under-tow of life still hadn't changed anything. Disgust filled her at her own inability to escape a past habit of reacting.

What was she going to say to big B? She wouldn't think about it, she would merely go there and blast him down and tell him to keep clear of Cordelia or else. . .

The birds were singing. She could hear the full rush

of their voices in the sycamores and the gnarled elderberry tree. What a clamour they were making!

Unable to sleep she got up. She would go down and make tea. Oh the problems of parenthood! 'Women,' she thought, 'are their own worst enemy. They don't work out strategies for dealing with life – they let emotion swamp them.'

She brewed a pot of tea, rolled another cigarette and then unlocked the back door and wandered out into the garden. It was veiled in a brownish twilight which made everything like an old sepia postcard.

Oh, but she was angry! She remembered the demise of the Rainbow Palace. It had left her feeling intensely impotent just as this was doing. Her instinctive reaction was to fight: being passive achieved nothing in situations like this. Cordelia had appeared tough to her – being brown had forced her to be a lot more hard-headed than most girls of her own age, and this was why it seemed so puzzling. Was it that she hadn't seen Cordelia clearly at all? Was it ever possible to learn from someone else's experience?

The whole thing defeated her – and yet she knew that it ought not to. She herself had rushed into one unsuitable liaison after another, being unable to resist the pull of the moment. Cordelia's father had been quite wrong for her – hectoring, lazy, he had expected a hand-maiden and she had rapidly tired of his demands whilst still being sexually in thrall. From moment to moment her attitude to him had changed, swinging from hatred to a sort of masochistic delight: she was being ground down. To snap off that awful, compulsive bond had taken much will-power. . .

She wandered towards the lamp-post which was resting on two blocks of wood, waiting for her to start work on it. About her loomed the chimney pots. Some had tulip heads, some crowns, some wizard shapes – they were the cowls. She had seen them as a girl towering against a pale evening sky and had been afraid. They must be symbols of some supernatural force. Her hand strayed down the length of the stone-coloured chimney pot whose only decoration was a faint dog-tooth marking around the rim. It felt smooth to her touch. At close quarters chimney pots assumed a potence which one would never have imagined, when one surveyed them from the ground and saw them perched aloft.

Turning, she looked up at the house and saw the light in Cordelia's bedroom. Evidently she too couldn't sleep. Ought she to go up? No – there was nothing to be said. She didn't feel she could bear to speak to her again at the moment. The worst of it was that she felt personally affronted by it – Cordelia couldn't have chosen anyone whom Linda could have disliked more. Was this merely adolescent rebellion against parental authority? If it were, then it was the more bizarre.

Linda turned away, remembering her tea. She saw her own mother's fury at the announcement that she was pregnant with Brenda. In those days couples had married as quickly as possible and it was referred to as 'a shot-gun wedding'. Jimmy had of course agreed – he hadn't had much chance. He'd been a year older and from the same sort of background as herself. You did what you were told by people in authority. She supposed her mother must have felt equally distraught – that caught her unawares: the repetitive nature of life was maddening. Trapped in the maze of unthought-out responses, Linda made her way back to the house.

Cordelia was sitting up in bed, a note book in front of her, writing. She wasn't sure what it was about even – she simply had to write, that was all. She couldn't understand the jumble of emotions. . . . Her mother had reacted just as she had expected her to, and it hadn't been any less horrific than she had imagined. When they both talked about it – her mother and Sue – they made it into something cold and threatening, which it was not. Whatever had happened between herself and Brocklesby was magic. They spoke as though it were degrading, ugly. . . . If only they could know the beauty of it. She wanted to set it down, word for word, explain. . .

Several hours later when Cordelia, wearing a cotton shift, was sitting at the kitchen table spooning muesli into her mouth, to the accompaniment of Radio 2, her mother emerged. She was decked out in combat gear, ex-army khaki trousers with camouflage top of green and brown which made her look like some immense boulder. Her frizzles of grey hair had been scraped back behind her head because of the heat. It was a glorious day outside, filled with the warbling of bullfinches and blackbirds and the chatter of starlings and sparrows.

Cordelia didn't know what to say so she kept her head down and continued eating, glad of the barrier of Jimmy Young. They weren't a household which went in for sulks. It was generally immense rages, screechings, door-slammings, wild floods of tears, a truce and then peace: but this was different, horribly different.

Linda made herself a cup of coffee and toasted a slice of bread. She would be going to the Emporium – you never could tell, there might be the odd customer, the fine weather was attracting people out onto the streets.

'Have you thought about what I said last night?' Linda began abruptly.

'Eh?'

'Turn that rabble off!'

Cordelia's finger depressed the on/off button. 'I said, have you thought about what I said?'

Silence filled with distant chirpings and the thunder of cars speeding to work.

'Well?'

'I don't want an abortion.'

'You're a fool, I'm telling you. You'll rue this till your dying day. I've seen too much of it.'

'Mum, you can't plan everything.'

'No, but you can make some attempt to see you experience some of the good things, they won't just drop in your lap, you know! The future isn't going to be rosy automatically – don't you see that? Youth's optimism is soon soured.'

Cordelia's face had closed in sullenness, it looked puffy and ancient. She was a West African fertility mask with bulging eye-balls, breasts and belly – both fierce and erotic in its starkness. Linda had seen such carvings at the British Museum.

'I don't care what's going to happen tomorrow – or next week for that matter –'

'That's patently obvious.'

'But if only you could see –'

'I can only too clearly.' Linda's mouth drew into a thin line, nipped down at the corners. 'I'm an old dog – you forget, I've seen too much –'

A dull stillness fell between them. 'Tonight I shall go round to see Brocklesby, I'll tell him my mind –' With that Linda wiped her mouth on the back of her hand, placed her plate and mug by the sink and stomped out. Cordelia put up a hand to smudge the sweat from her nose and forehead. Why had her life got to end in disaster? Wasn't it possible that events could simply be changed by your way of taking them?

That day seemed to pass very slowly for Cordelia.

She spent most of it, either lying in a deckchair under the shade of the elderberry tree and flicking away the black mites which cascaded onto her face periodically, or in her bedroom, writing in her exercise books. She had made up her mind that she would go round to Brocklesby's house in the early evening and warn him of her mother's intentions. On no account did she want to bump into Linda again before she left.

Cordelia walked to Brocklesby's house. It was so warm that she had to saunter. Her armpits felt damp, her palms sweated. The heat was causing her feet to swell. The lines of sycamores met overhead and formed a light green arch. Light swam on the dark grey road in liquid lemon shapes, always forming and re-forming. She hadn't allowed herself yet to feel glad about what was happening to her body. When she wasn't fighting off nausea, a certain deep enjoyment was beginning to assert itself – the whole of her was starting to grow rounder.

Brocklesby soon came to the door. She thought of a scene in a hall-way with her dress unbuttoned from neck to hem, her body against his suit and that had been the most erotic thing in the world, a swift spear of excitement.

'Hello.' There was a query in his eyes.

'I had to tell you my Mum's going to come round this evening. I've said I'm pregnant – you can imagine what she's like –'

'Yes,' he said, 'I can.'

They went into the drawing room. 'I can't make her understand –' Cordelia broke off. 'She seems to think it's all such a tragedy and so gloomy – and it's not.'

'If you look at me like that, I might want to –'

'Mm, well, I might want to in any case – except that my mother'll be knocking at the door any minute.'

'Does she know you'll be here?'

'No.'

'What do you want me to do?'

There wasn't time to do anything because the door-bell sounded.

'Oh Christ –' Cordelia's heart thumped. Her body was engulfed in a wave of sweat.

'Wait here!'

'You know why I've come?'

Cordelia shuddered, hearing her mother's voice and then Brocklesby's lower tones.

'Yes, I do. Come in.'

'I ought to say what I've got to say on the street –' Linda was further enraged by the very sight of him, her old adversary over the years. She was back at the time of the Rainbow Palace, seeing the bulldozers flattening her tall, thin slice of house and leaving nothing – how impotent she felt! She had no means of getting even with him.

Against her will, she caught herself glancing about her at his treasures. You had to admit, he had some fine stuff.

With an unpleasant shock she saw Cordelia sitting in an armchair.

'What are you doing here?'

Cordelia's honesty took her breath away. 'I thought I'd better warn him –' There was no answer to that one. She found herself smiling grimly.

'A drink?'

'Drink? Certainly not, I've not come to that yet –'

'But you might?' Brocklesby said, and something like a grin twitched at his lips.

'Never. You did this just to spite me, didn't you?' Linda was standing in the centre of the room staring venomously at Brocklesby who was leaning on the mantlepiece.

187

'No,' he said, 'it's just incidental that she's your daughter, I just happened to like her.'

'She's a kid! If I –' she stopped abruptly, wondering at what she was about to say. 'You ought to be horse-whipped!' That was the sort of thing her mother had said to Jimmy. 'If I were a man –'

'I admit I should have known better –'

'I'm surprised you can even bring yourself so far as to do that. I really am amazed!'

Brocklesby was evidently beginning to lose patience with the scene and his eyes had taken on a threatening gleam.

'And what exactly is the purpose of your visit?'

'Just to tell you I think you're a louse. And you'd better keep away from her – that's it as far as I'm concerned. You're a dirty louse –'

'And you're an evil-mouthed old cow!'

'Thanks for that!'

They were both glancing at each other, their faces twisted in spite, Brocklesby's caught in a sardonic rictus. Cordelia could hardly bear it. Almost unconscious of what she was doing, she interposed herself physically between them.

'Oh Christ, you two, stop it. You're both old enough to know better – can't you see how silly it is? I'm pregnant – so – you're carrying on as though it's a national disaster. People get pregnant every day – do be sensible!' She seized hold of each of them by the arm. The tension seemed to snap. There was a most peculiar feeling. 'Smile at each other, stop snarling, do, for my sake!'

Brocklesby and Linda stood woodenly like two small children, uncertain what to do. 'Come on,' Cordelia insisted, 'apologise to each other, Mum – Dale –'

'All right – all right,' Brocklesby said, 'I didn't mean

188

to call you an old –'

'Hm, well – I can't think how we let her get us into this –'

'Don't bother analysing it –' Cordelia pressed on. 'Please say you'll stop dogging each other. Life can be magic but you've got to let it be. It won't be if you don't believe. You seem to think that magic, if there ever were to be any would drop down from above –'

Somehow they found themselves sitting with drinks in their hands. Brocklesby's gory head was not being carried out on a platter.

'She says she won't have an abortion.'

'I want to marry her –'

'Well, I think I'll just go on living with Mum, if you don't mind, but I'll keep popping round to see you –'

'But I would really have liked to – don't you understand?'

'Never mind –' Cordelia closed the matter, almost primly.

Talk inevitably veered to the tat and antique business. As Cordelia had previously surmised, the older people shared a great deal in common.

'She's actually after the shop in George Street,' Cordelia said, grinning, still buoyed up by a burst of peculiar energy, which was driving her on and refusing to let her be overcome by fear. 'Are you going to sell it to Mum at a reasonable price?'

Brocklesby looked at Cordelia in real admiration. 'You're a little demon, really,' he said.

'Well, are you?'

'Cordelia, for goodness sake, you're embarrassing me – I just don't know –' For the first time in years Linda actually found herself blushing.

'All right,' Brocklesby said, 'let's bury the hatchet by agreeing to some reasonable figure.'

189

They had another couple of drinks and all three of them considered it to have been one of the strangest evenings in their lives.

Chapter 21

Sue went to work the next day, after the catastrophe of Cordelia's pregnancy had been revealed, feeling quite light-headed. What a contrary business life was, she thought as she strode along the back streets towards the college. In her own school days one girl had become pregnant when they were in the Lower Sixth and it had been regarded as a dreadful scandal, which had kept them entertained for several days. Mary Skelton had disappeared not long after the news had broken. It had seemed, she remembered, like an act of God – being of the same nature as such natural disasters as earthquakes and fires. They had all dreamed of Mary and her lover, the plumbing apprentice, seeing in them some Laurentian short story. Of course it was much later that Sue had arrived at her final denunciation of Lawrence. One day, months later, she had met Mary in the street and Mary had been pushing a pram. She hadn't looked at all wild and romantic, but somehow very ordinary and fatter – and the baby? She had forgotten about it until that moment – the baby had appeared unformed, reddish and rather spotty. Mary and the baby had been a disappointment to her and she had preferred to lose them in her memory's lumber-room.

What if all this led to a permanent rift between Linda and Cordelia? The thought troubled Sue. She couldn't imagine the scene between Linda and Brocklesby – she just hoped it wouldn't end in physical violence.

It was weird how one minute everything was jogging alone pleasantly enough, and the next a disaster had occurred. Once you began to speculate on the arbitrary nature of events, it could become quite daunting.

As usual she chuntered to herself about the choking blue exhaust fumes puffing out from the lines of Maxis, Volvos and Fiats, all with their Union Jack and Falklands' stickers affixed to their back windows.

She made it across the road and the pelican crossing, expecting to be ploughed under the wheels of some carbon-monoxide-spewing monster at any second. Passing in front of the hospital gates, she saw the pickets' placards proclaiming the NUPE strike. A group of men and women were sitting and standing about in a rather embarrassed way as though they felt they were giving some amateur theatrical production for which they must apologise. They caused her to feel embarrassed as well because of their own obvious discomfort.

It was, she reflected, a very tense time of the year – it suggested 'Finals', 'A' Levels, 'O' Levels, mornings and afternoons spent in cold halls writing at top speed or pausing now and then and thinking you simply couldn't go on. This generally coincided with halcyon days outside, temperatures in the seventies and the sun blazing on tarmac turning it to goo.

Even though your own examination days were past, you re-lived them every year through each new generation of students. She saw them clutching rulers, pens, biros and tubes of Polos and fruit gums, some silent and withdrawn, others giggling to hide their nervousness.

192

It was also the time for bitter staff feuding. This gained momentum throughout the summer term. All their frustrations emerged gradually, their feelings of having missed out and of having been over-looked in the promotion stakes. Words like 'arse-licker' were bandied around. Sometimes there were battles over classrooms: you might find your customary room had been taken over for an exam without your having been notified of the change.

'I'm not moving – I've been here the entire year!'

'You've got to – the examination has to go on.'

'I shan't move these boys out.' Twenty or so hulking apprentices would drum their skin-head boots good-humouredly on the floor until the ancient planking vibrated. (These skirmishes invariably erupted in far-flung annexes which were out of reach of the long claw of authority.)

Outside the room door groups of sweating students would be eyeing developments nervously, they just wanted to be able to do their 'A' Level Law in peace.

After fifteen or so minutes of haranguing, the offending class generally withdrew, irritably kicking the tubular metal chair-legs and lugging huge sports bags, to another class-room. But that wouldn't be the end of it, because later the two teachers concerned would snarl at each other.

Sue wondered if little Jesperson would have filled her pigeon-hole with memos. At this point he generally went quite crazy. 'Martin Jesperson to Sue Edwards Gen. Cat. IC exam not now on June 14th. Change to June 24th. Let me have copies of exam papers plus exam scripts.' Such made her fume – what did that little wormy Jesperson think he was doing? Jesperson came up to her navel, was bright and bouncy and a little sucker, he specialised in General Studies. She hated the way he focused on her crotch and frisked about her. At one period he had taken to dropping in. For what purpose she wasn't clear.

The work-room smelt of smoke, but was empty. You could still feel the presence of the people who had just left it. Her eye took in the usual list of petitions. Had she signed them? There was the one supporting the UN Special Session on Disarmament, the Anti-Apartheid, the one against the Neutron Bomb.

Reluctantly she turned to the orange plastic pigeon-holes. Of course there must be! Jesperson had sent her another memo. 'M. Jesperson to S. Edwards. Discount earlier communication. GI exams now June 17th – same rules apply re papers.

Sue cursed to herself and dumped 'M. Jesperson to S. Edwards' in the metal wastebin. She approached the tea-table where the electric kettle and the cups stood. The cups with their interesting mould cultures were still piled up there, despite the head of department's note, or rather perhaps because of it. But now a new note had appeared. It was a placard. 'This must be removed at once' by order of the Caretaker.

Just then Marina Dewsbury, Principal Lecturer, barrelled in.

'Look at that! My, it wouldn't have been allowed in the last college I taught in in Canada. Janitors jolly well kept their place. I mean it's not their place to instruct us about our cups. We'll have the cleaning women taking over soon.'

She drifted out bearing piles of questionnaires. Sue made herself a cup of coffee and slid into her seat at the work-bench, determined to mark a few General Studies exam papers.

This was the time when the old Hamish business had flowered – always the last few weeks of a dying session.

194

He would be sitting there beside her and now and then they'd exchange a glance or a word with the knowledge that they were bound for her flat later in the afternoon – and that had been rather exciting. Now he would be making his big pots and growing beans and courgettes in the back garden – not a bad life, but she didn't envy him.

Before she knew it, lunch-time had arrived. Poor Cordelia – she'd 'phone the theatre group later in the day and see if there was any response to her play. Martin Jesperson bounced in. He walked with splayed feet, emphasised by his Doc Martin boots. They made him look like Charlie Chaplin.

'Hi Sue, lunch?'

Caught off her guard, she agreed. They went through into the refectory. Sue strode before him whilst he bounded at her heels, grinning widely.

'What's been occurring in your world, Sue?' he asked, beaming as they faced each other over their salad sandwiches and pale tea.

'Just irritations like getting your memos.'

'Oh gee, Sue, don't let that get you down – I'm awful sorry –'

Jesperson had lived in America and he talked with a nasal twang.

'Well they do – and when you've finished, I'm never sure what I'm supposed to do at all.'

Scrunch, Jesperson's teeth went into his bread cake and the lettuce shot out at one side and he hastily tried to push it back.

'So how's life, Sue?'

'Exciting, stimulating, brilliant –'

'Hey, gee, Sue, tell me more!'

'The exotic, erotic, rave life of Sue F. Edwards!'

'That sounds mighty good to me – what, what?'

'Yes, you'd like to know, wouldn't you. Well what about your life?' Sue fixed him with big aquamarine eyes and a mocking smile.

'Oh gee, there's Ted. I'd – would you mind if I had a word?'

'I couldn't care a fuck!' Sue said, tossing back her hair and stroking it behind an ear, 'no I couldn't –'

Jesperson rose and scuttled off, looking hurt and alarmed. Sue felt she wanted to laugh uproariously but restrained herself as she feared it would sound eccentric.

After finishing her sandwich, she wandered back to the work-room, delved in her bag for a red biro and started making corrections in the margins of essays, an underlining here, a balloon there. After a certain number of scripts it all became quite mechanical.

Suddenly the work-room door opened. She didn't look up. She was wrestling with a complicated sentence which appeared to contain no finite verb, only a scattering of present participles.

'Same scene several months later!' a voice said.

Sue's head jerked up with surprise.

'My God, it's Jim Dacre!'

'The very one.' His worn face grinned.

Sue pushed her chair back and stared at him. 'What on earth are you doing here?'

'Come for an interview for a job at the Binnington F.E. College, so I thought I'd drop in and see what was happening here. After all the Binnington place is only a mere eight miles away!'

'Did you come anywhere?'

'Got it – bloody got it, how about that? After three years of temps, I've actually netted a full-time job.'

Sue was currently in a smoking period and she began

196

to make a roll-up. He had hauled himself up onto the work-bench and was watching her.

'I'm very pleased for you.'

'Tell me the latest about you!'

She had forgotten how eager he was and how his enthusiasm for life won people immediately. All she could do was swing back in her chair and grin.

'House owner, owner of a vast number of valuable objects d'art, of a garden which actually produces courgettes, potatoes, rhubarb, parsley. I've been having a nesting phase, and a reading phase.'

'Men?'

'Oh, they come and go. I've decided fantasy is better than their reality.'

'Bad, very bad.'

'Catastrophically bad.' She grinned wider. 'Hey Jim, it's good to see you, all jokes aside.'

'Ditto.'

'What's with you then?'

'Divorced – that's been pretty grim. I'm just relieved it's over – and I've been doing temporary lecturing whenever I could get it, nothing fantastic.'

They talked about the time when he'd been replacing Harry, about Hamish and others who had disappeared from the scene.

'Life's quite a tough business,' Jim remarked. 'We've got a cushy number, though compared with a lot of folks. Up in the north east where I come from there's hardly a family without someone unemployed in it. You should see the resorts up the coast, just going to seed, everything crumbling. My old Mum and Dad have lived through it all before.'

He asked her what time she'd be finishing and what about a quick drink before the pubs closed. As she wasn't scheduled to teach, she went with him.

197

Side by side they walked down the long corridor flanked by work-shops. The carpentry shop hummed with saws and drills. Boys were planing and lovely curls of blond wood were piling up near the benches and everybody looked engrossed. Lower down youths were welding with oxyacetylene torches and arcs of brilliant light flickered on metal shields. The area reeked of fumes.

The sunlight dazzled them as they emerged. 'Hey, I really *am* glad to see you!' Jim grinned as the pelican crossing peeped, and they went into the George Hotel opposite the main college building.

They looked at each other and laughed – it seemed amazingly good fortune.

'I never thought I'd see you here again. I thought you'd disappeared into the maw for good.'

'No, I was determined to come back.'

She didn't ask him the reason.

In the cool gloom of the pub with the Space Invader's siren calls and the juke boxes booming and tinkling so loudly they could scarcely hear each other speak, they ordered halves of lager and selected a corner table.

'To your new job!'

'Thanks. Tell me about your nesting place!'

'Well, I've had immense pleasure, painting, decorating, learning to do all manner of things – plastering for one, and then gardening – I never thought I would – but this place is very satisfying.' She didn't tell him about her baby-dreams, because they had passed. Tracy Pittaway had effectively killed the phase for her and it was now part of her private world: you were strong in the things you didn't share.

After the half pints they went, on impulse, for a stroll through the Old Town, because Jim had an urge to go down to the pierhead where the ferry used to ply across the estuary, churning over to Lincolnshire.

When they were standing in the hot afternoon looking out across the water, seeing that vast, softly undulating gun-metal mass, he turned to her, 'I used to come here often,' he said softly, 'last time when I was up here. I'd sit on one of those benches and just watch the water. It was very calming – you know I was all stewed up about whether or not Jane and I had finished and what about our kid. I knew we'd nothing in common, didn't even like each other, but it seemed such a hell of a step, and now it's passed, everything passes –'

'Yes,' she said, knowing it was the truth and that it was both a consolation and a dread.

'It's so peaceful – and when you think of those young guys dying –'

'Yes,' she said again, 'it's all the emotive words that fire people – like "fatherland", "my country" just romanticism and dreams. But how can you totally escape, eh?'

He grinned at her and wrinkled up his forehead. She looked into his grey striped eyes. 'I'll tell you straight up, you can't, not completely – you can try, but –'

At the rail, he halted and leaned his elbows on it. She sat on one of the wooden forms and let the breeze riffle through her hair and lie coolly on her cheeks. When you looked at the bare statistics, like twenty million Russian soldiers dead in the last war, your head reeled and you couldn't attempt to grasp what those figures meant in terms of human grief and folly, all those grieving millions of mothers who had reared children. and for what?

They remained as they were for an indefinite time and then he came across to where she was sitting and sat down beside her. He put his hand on hers and turned her face sideways so that he could kiss her on the mouth.

When they broke apart, Sue's cheeks were very

pink and she was breathing rapidly. 'This is another still,' she thought, remembering the previous evening in the garden watching the secret beauty of the summer moon over the backs. She was aware of each detail of Jim Dacre's face – the lined forehead, the sexy eyes, and the mouth, the strong, square teeth: a little wiry, weaselly man with a hard body and not much flesh, a Northerner.

'We're old campaigners,' he said smiling.

'Yes,' she agreed, knowing that they were indeed both well-versed in the ways of men and women; they had visited the familiar battle-grounds and experienced labour-disputes which invariably ended in savagery.

'It takes you a long time to get over the realisation that feelings change and that the things you thought you'd never forget, you do, and what appeared as inessentials remain with you – particularly for someone like me from a working-class background. You married the lass-next-door, had kids, rowed but stayed the course – you know like Andy Capp.'

They got up and wandered along the dockside for a while, looking at the old lock-gates and the silted-up waterway. It smelt of bladderwrack and salt and of something far flung and indefinable.

'Do you want to come to my house and have tea in the garden?'

'I'd like that.'

They went on foot all the way back to her street. The heat made them sweat but now and then a breeze brought some relief. Jim Dacre was wearing his interview suit. He shed the jacket as soon as he entered the house.

'Really, Sue, this is bloody lovely. I can see what you mean – your own home that you've worked for –'

'Yes, I just take a delight in each bit of it. I used to

200

feel guilty vaguely because here I am, enjoying things like tea-pots when everywhere there's death and mayhem – but I've passed that stage.'

'Yes,' he said, looking out at the ivy.

'I suppose maybe I terrify a lot of people because I'm doing my own thing and I don't compromise. Are you terrified of me, Jim Dacre?'

'Yes, I'm utterly emasculated!'

'Where would you like tea? In my magic garden?'

'As long as there's a bit of shade.'

Sue looked into his face and then he wasn't smiling. 'Come here, you giantess, I want to kiss you –'

Their tea was left to cool and somehow they mounted her stairway and ended up in her bedroom. She found that she was almost afraid because it had been a very long time since she had been with a man. He sensed her diffidence and he undid the buttons on her shirt and kissed her throat – and sometimes they grinned at each other, finding it all very funny.

'Do you think your cock can manage a massive lady like me?' she joked.

'It'll have a damned good try.'

He seemed to ramble over her, nimble, knotty, above all sexy. She could feel the urgency in him and she cradled him against her. They lay sideways their mouths sucking and their hands touching the flesh of back, shoulders, buttocks. He had small, hard buttocks and they felt like moons in her hands.

The breeze from the street coming in through the open window caused the beads on the dressing-table wing-mirror to tremble and tinkle delightfully and the beaded light-shades clinked. Eros gleamed, as though covered in oil or water, in the afternoon sunlight. The room was rich, ruined exotic. She put her legs

201

round his neck and laughing and serious he thrust down into her. She gave a great gasp and moaned.

They finally reached the garden a long time later. He was wearing her black satin kimono with the red dragon snarling on its back and was otherwise naked.

'That was very, very good!' he said.

'I feel,' she said, 'as though I could become quite obsessional about you.'

'Good.'

'I don't know that it is – I suppose it's better to keep each other at a distance and take it slowly –'

They sat there for a long time, watching the pond's surface quiver and listening to the bullfinches and blackbirds. Within the confines of the garden which was caught between two high hedges, the perfume of the yellow tea roses was very strong. He drank his tea and kept a hand on her thigh, so that she could feel the heat of his fingers through the thin cotton of her shift.

'Why have you never married?' he asked.

'It's not something I see in my scheme of things . . . I don't think I could live easily with someone else.'

'No . . .'

He stayed on. They wandered down the road in the twilight and bought a Chinese take-away and some bottles of lager and then they sat at her kitchen table and ate the bean-shoots, chicken, mushrooms and rice in a leisurely way and stared at the light shining on the ivy leaves outside.

'I ought to have gone to Birmingham on the train – but it'll have to be first thing in the morning as it is.'

The evening drifted by and was spent mostly in Sue's bedroom. It had no demarcations and one thing flowed into another. Sometimes they were kissing, sometimes chatting. The past and present interwove. She exchanged her life for his and it was fun to watch where

202

they overlapped and what were similarities and what differences. It was like visiting an unknown country. You never knew what you might discover.

'It's the things like irritability and intolerance and aggressiveness in men that I find difficult to take – the ever-demanding ego which has to be fed.'

'Yes – I'm from a home where Dad came in from work and there was his tea on the table and then it was off to the pub for a pint – and things like that are ingrained in you –'

'Why did it fail with Jane?'

'All sorts of things. But she was very tidy and liked order and planning and couldn't be spontaneous, and I'm impulsive, disorderly, wanting to do things on the spur of the moment – and you see, you build up a series of arguments over the years and then it's as though you merely have to press a button and they all come hurtling out and you're locked into a certain way of reacting – and we only had to set eyes on each other to start. You know, 'Oh I wish you wouldn't put that there!' 'I do wish you wouldn't say that!' 'You don't *have* to say such things?' 'Why did you leave the top off the jam-pot?' Basically it all comes down to a lack of tolerance. Then you start looking about for other people and fancying them.'

'The joys of marriage!' Sue rolled over on her stomach and looked at the ceiling. He ran his fingertips down her spine.

'Don't get me wrong. I think it can be bloody marvellous – it's a kind of lovely certainty when it's going all right.'

Sue wondered vaguely why they were talking about marriage.

He stayed the night and she kept waking up and being amazed and thrilled to see the little wiry man

203

beside her – and often he was awake too and he'd run his fingertips over her breasts and stroke her belly and reach for the opening, touching her so gently and then he'd move over her again, or they'd lie side by side and once he was at her back with his arms round her waist and sometimes she lay on top of him and they'd laugh because she'd ask him whether she was crushing him.

When he left the following morning very early, she could hardly bear it. She didn't go with him to the door because she didn't want to see him walking down that long street, carrying his battered briefcase.

'I'll be back Saturday,' he'd said, but somehow she hadn't believed it.

She went back into the bedroom and looked at the side of the bed where he had slept, at the pillow where his head had lain. She sniffed at the sheets in an attempt to recapture his smell. Her body felt sticky and smelt of his semen and between her legs it was sore. Then she remembered that for fifteen hours or so she had not once thought of the predicament which had befallen Cordelia and Linda.

In the kitchen was the mug from which he had drunk his tea and a plate with the toast crumbs like fine sand upon it – those were reminders that he had really been.

Chapter 22

'I feel like a goon in this,' Linda remarked, poking her head round Cordelia's door. Cordelia, who was posing before the mirror, in a bright blue cotton shift and some matching shoes and big blue plastic earrings, looked at her mother in surprise. Linda had put on a 1920s crêpe dress which draped her ample figure in a series of diagonal swathes.

'I've never seen you in a dress before.'

'Well,' Linda said crossly, 'don't draw attention to it. I've told you, I feel an idiot – Christ, the thing that got washed up by the sea!'

'Mum, stop it!'

'I don't know what's come over Sue . . . we'd best hurry, come on –'

They went downstairs into the living room where Robin and Tom were waiting. Linda had taken on Robin as her assistant in the new shop, an arrangement which suited them both admirably.

'Isn't this absolutely hilarious!' Tom said and did a tap dance. He had just dyed his hair a whiter blond and was wearing his best drop-earring, a huge imitation pearl, depending from two smaller ones linked with a silver chain. Robin had re-hennaed his hair in honour of the occasion.

When Linda entered they both let out whoops and Linda pulled one of her most hideous faces.

'What time's Big B. arriving?' she wanted to know.

'Any minute.'

'Where the hell are the bride and groom?'

'Still in bed I shouldn't wonder –' Tom gave out.

Just then there was a blast on the door-bell and Sue, Jim and Brocklesby entered.

'Coo, I like that!' Cordelia said. Sue was wearing a 1920s black crêpe suit and white ruffled blouse and aquamarine earrings, long drops which took up the colour of her eyes. Jim was grinning broadly in his interview suit. Brocklesby, immaculate as usual in his navy-blue pinstripe suit, handed out white carnations all round and Sue gave him a kiss on the cheek.

'All set?'

'My God, we're going to have a ride in the princely chariot!' Sue exclaimed. 'Don't go too fast – I hate cars – I suppose Jags are more civilized than most.'

They all packed into the white Jaguar, grinning and spluttering and cramming onto each other's knees – and Sue had to have Jim on hers.

'Don't squash my carnation, you!'

'I'll go splat, right in the middle of it!'

'Hey, do you think we're doing the right thing?'

'Yes – only don't you expect heaven, there'll be good bits and a lot of rotten stuff as well and we'll be bloody nasty and pissed off at times . . . but –'

'But, but –'

'Oh, it's too late now,' Linda rumbled. She was almost expiring between Robin and Tom. 'Boys have such hard legs!' she remarked. She was feeling delighted with the way the lamp-post had turned out and Big B. had been most helpful in the carrying of

206

effects for the shop. Yes, she could almost say that – well, basically he was quite decent. She – yes – she did like him.

They lined up in the registrar's office, big Sue, and Jim who reached up to her shoulder, and they were clutching hands and grinning at each other in an absurd way. And never was there such a peacock's array of colour. Cordelia loved it. She gasped as she felt the baby give a big flip in her tummy, and Brocklesby grasped her hand. She thought of that evening when they were going to see her play performed by 'Women's Wiles' at the Arts Centre. It was all so exciting that she could hardly attend to what was happening. She wanted to rush onto the next bit and devour it.

And Sue, as she walked out of the registry office which faced the glass tooth where she taught, felt a great surge of emotion. Here were the people she loved. She took hold of Linda's arm and squeezed it and put an arm round Cordelia and Jim. 'Pity Mum and Dad couldn't have come.' They were on holiday in Ireland. Over the telephone her mother had sounded most surprised. 'But Sue, are you sure – is that what you really want? I thought –' And Sue had said, 'I've no idea, it just came –'

Indeed, she reflected, as they trekked along, laughing and falling off the edge of the kerb and smelling exhaust fumes and watching the white clouds scudding in the sky and the sun blazing, the beauty of life was its refusal to be ordered or planned in any way. Things happened, and mourning alternated with rejoicing, and underlying the whole was this same extreme unpredictability. No doubt, when you died it would happen in the same way. Cordelia was right, in order to experience magic, you had to believe in it.

If you have enjoyed this book and would like to receive
details of other Piatkus publications please write to

Judy Piatkus (Publishers) Limited
Loughton
Essex